# Holiday Abduction

By
Eve Langlais
*(Alien Abduction #6)*

# Copyright and Disclaimer

Copyright © November 2014, Eve Langlais
Cover Art by Amanda Kelsey © November 2014
Edited by Devin Govaere
Copy Edited by Amanda L. Pederick
Produced in Canada

Published by Eve Langlais
1606 Main Street, PO Box 151
Stittsville, Ontario, Canada, K2S1A3
http://www.EveLanglais.com

ISBN-13: 978-1503016491
ISBN-10: 1503016498

# Chapter One

*"Never forget they're always watching. And they see everything. It's why I line my bras with tin foil." –*
*Grandma's philosophy on alien life.*

The end of the world didn't happen.

Another wish dashed.

Staring at the sky didn't produce a horde of alien spacecraft about to invade Earth, but as if to mock her, the most delicate of snowflakes tumbled from the clouds overhead. Without a breeze, each sparkling mote drifted down to coat the ground in an innocent layer, which tormented her.

Logically, Jilly knew she shouldn't blame the land. It wasn't the farm's fault she was so damned screwed. Instead, she should condemn those stupid pencil pushers in their cubicles at the bank who seemed to think that today's economy and lack of employment weren't their problem. Well, it was, and hers too if she didn't find a way to make some cash, and quick.

Only a few days before Christmas and less than a week until the mortgage came due, along with all the penalties she'd accrued from missed and late payments. If she didn't pay the sums owing in full, she stood to lose her home, which totally sucked. Of all her aspirations in life, homelessness didn't number among them.

Was it any wonder she'd kind of hoped for a

solar flare that would wipe out all the computers in the world leaving her with more time to figure out where she would find the money to make ends meet?

One thing was for sure. She wouldn't find any money on the farm.

The orchard with its stunted apple trees, which had barely produced any fruit the last two years, wouldn't suddenly leaf green bills.

The field infested with butterfly larva wouldn't suddenly sprout a crop she could use.

And the restaurant she used to work at wasn't likely to reopen its doors and give her back her job, not with the scathing report the health inspector wrote. Mario, the owner, should have never broken up with Marianne. She didn't take the rejection well.

Perhaps Jilly could pull the money from her ass. More like by shaking her ass. With things down to the wire, there weren't many options left to make a few grand quick, unless she got naked. For strangers.

Shudder.

*There has to be a better way.* Something she could sell other than her body. But what?

The house contained relics of a bygone era, but she wouldn't exactly call them antiques. Somehow she doubted butt-ugly furniture from the seventies and cracked knickknacks—glued a few too many times—would find many buyers. Heck, given the state of some of the stuff, she'd probably have to pay to get it taken away.

As Jilly continued to stare at the sky, still not giving up hope that an alien invasion would target her bank, she noted a bright spot streaking through the low hanging, cloud layer.

A shooting star?

Should she take it as a positive omen?

*Quick. Make a wish.*

She closed her eyes tight as she whispered words that only the falling snow could hear. "Help me find a way to have a Merry Christmas." And a Happy New Year where she wasn't homeless.

Fervent plea made, she opened her eyes, and her jaw dropped open as she gaped. Perhaps she should have wished to keep her house instead because the falling star seemed intent on colliding with it. The brilliant spot, instead of winking harmlessly out of sight, appeared to be headed straight toward her.

Much like the dumb deer—whom she took potshots at when they came to nibble on her crops—she stared at the bright light. She wasn't stupid enough to think she could outrun it or that hiding inside would save her. Not at the speed the shooting meteor traveled and the size, which grew from a speck to a boulder to the size and shape of a…coffin?

Closing her eyes and reopening them did nothing to change her perception. It still looked like a bloody sarcophagus.

Creepy. Especially since it slowed right down and parked itself gently and upright on her front lawn.

While happy the flying tomb didn't smash into her or the house, somehow she wasn't completely reassured.

*If this were a horror movie, then what comes next probably won't be good for my general health.*

Foreboding formed a ball in her stomach, and she ran inside the house to grab the shotgun. As she wrapped her hand around the familiar wooden stock, she could almost hear her departed grandma say, *"Jilly, if it don't look right, fetch the gun."*

Actually, Grandma's solution to most problems involved fetching a weapon, loaded with custom-made silver bullets because as Grandma said, *"Always be prepared for anything, Jilly-bean. Just because we ain't never seen a werewolf doesn't mean they're not lurking out there."*

With crazy advice like that, as well as the garlic strung over every window, the salt Grandma kept pouring around the perimeter of the house and the aluminum they went through every month, was it any wonder why Jilly canceled Grandma's issue of 'True Believers Wear Tin Foil Hats'? Cousin Betty stopped talking to her after that, as if it was Jilly's fault Grandma was her only subscriber.

Uttering a silent apology to both her cousin and grandma, whom it seemed might have been right when they claimed life was out there—and waiting to enslave all women as sex slaves—Jilly thanked the fact she knew how to shoot.

With Problem Solver in hand—the name she gave her gun when gifted to her on her twenty-first birthday—Jilly stood on her front porch wearing pink, tattered bunny-eared slippers, baggy red plaid, flannel pants, a snug T-shirt that read 'Ray of fucking sunshine' and a blanket around her shoulders because it was winter after all. As outfits went, she wouldn't win any prizes unless it was how to not impress possible alien life when it landed on your doorstep.

If it was an alien.

Perhaps the strange object was some kind of government drone thing. Those money-spending, tax-collecting jerks were always wasting funds on stupid projects.

But if it was them, why were they visiting her farm at nine o'clock at night?

The giant coffin sat there, attempting to appear innocuous but not succeeding. It surprised her to note that the snow at its base didn't hiss or steam. Obviously it used some kind of propulsion system, but of a sort that didn't emit heat. Weird.

*Or a sign it's not from this world.* She could practically hear Grandma cackle in glee at the thought.

Cradling her gun in her arms, Jilly studied the vessel, trying to pigeonhole it into something comprehensible, but it seemed determined to thwart her.

Snow didn't stick or melt upon it. Instead, it drifted down around the object, leaving its surface untouched. The impression of a large coffin only increased as she looked at it, but not the modern day rectangular kind, more like those they unearthed from ancient Egyptian tombs, except this one lacked markings and appeared a uniform, metallic gray.

No lights shone from any one spot, and yet the surface itself appeared to emit some kind of glow. Odd, almost as odd as the lack of seams and despite the fact it flew in as if guided, she didn't hear any kind of engine noise. Nothing.

Could she totally hear *Twilight Zone* music playing in her head? Fucking right she did, and it didn't help she heard her dead grandma saying, *"I told you they'd come one day."*

A pity the woman who raised her wasn't around to see it. She'd have probably baked one of her famous seven layer cakes—with real to-die-for buttercream icing—to celebrate.

When the coffin decided, with just the tiniest of clicks as warning, to split open, she didn't know what to expect. Friendly and cute, bobble head, green Martian saying, "I come in peace", or slavering monster with great big fangs and slimy, warty skin intent on seeing if human flesh was a delicacy?

Given the possibilities, was it any wonder Jilly raised her shotgun and aimed it at the exposed interior?

But as the interior was exposed, along with its occupant, she didn't fire, although she did stare in slack-jawed disbelief.

*I'll be damned. Grandma was right.*

There was life out there. And it was a heck of a lot sexier than expected.

Bright blue eyes, that held a hint of a glow, met her brown gaze and studied her intently. Up.

Down. He—had to be a male with that square jaw, strong nose, and masculine build—didn't disguise his perusal of her, and she fought an urge to fidget. When the alien—because no human ever sported purple skin like this dude—raised a dark brow and smirked, she straightened her spine.

She also channeled the corniest line in known cinema. "Come out with your hands up."

"And if I don't?" The reply, spoken in a low, silken tone, took her aback.

"You speak English?"

"I speak and understand every language in the known universe thanks to my upgraded thought-to-speech voice modulator. But that is of no import. You have yet to answer my first question. What will you do if I do not exit my surface pod?"

Grandma would have advocated shooting first, asking questions later, but Jilly preferred to think violence wasn't always the only answer. Which led her to another thing Grandma always said. *"Men always think with their bellies."* Did that apply to galactic invaders too?

"Stay in your pod thing if you want. But it will be your loss because I've got fresh, oven-baked cookies and hot cocoa." Without the arsenic her grandma might have laced it with if she wasn't too crazy about the company coming over.

Living with Grandma, who went a little insane after Grandpa died, Jilly dumped more than her fair share of suspected beverages and snacks. She'd learned her lesson after Timmy dared to sneak a kiss, Timmy being a boy Grandma did not approve of, given he had no goals in life. Luckily all he ended up with was an upset stomach, but Jilly learned to watch Grandma carefully after that.

Back to her alien guest and roundabout offer to come in for cookies and cocoa. She didn't wait for a reply. She turned on her heel and walked back into the house.

Lest anyone think she was nonchalant about the situation, her heart raced so fast she feared a coronary. Her hands, despite the outdoor chill, sweated enough to make her grip on the gun slick, and the only reason she hadn't peed herself was because she clenched her Kegels so tight she'd attained virgin status again.

Yet she let none of her trepidation show. She attempted to treat her unexpected visitor with a bit of trust because *I damn well don't want it said that I started an alien invasion because I was trigger-happy.*

Determination to not make history didn't mean she was completely stupid. The gun stayed with her as she strode down the straight hall to her kitchen. Any second, she expected to go up in a vaporized puff of smoke. Instead, she heard the click of her front door closing.

*Great. I invited a giant alien inside. Now what?*

Feed him before he fed on her.

*I hope he likes chocolate chip cookies and not chocolate-dipped humans.*

# Chapter Two

*"If you want it, take it." The first rule from the most stolen book in the universe, The Fine Art of Acquisition. A must read for all serious collectors.*

Vhyl wondered why he bothered to follow the barbarian female. It certainly wasn't because she offered food. He'd already eaten before embarking on this planet-side mission.

He couldn't have claimed it was out of fear. Vhyl feared nothing, especially not a female sporting archaic combustion-based weaponry, not to mention his surface exploring garb was fabricated of material capable of resisting most missiles and laser fire.

So why did he follow the wiggle of her hips and the dark, curly hair that bounced down her back?

Because he wanted to.

And Vhyl wasn't one to question or deny himself anything.

If he coveted it, he took it. If he admired it, he stole it. If he wanted to delay his current mission slightly to follow an intriguing barbarian female into her abode and admire, at greater length, her dual mammary glands encased in the tight thin fabric that did nothing to hide the erectness of her nipples, then he would.

If she intrigued him enough, he might even

take her with him when he left.

They didn't call him the Black Hole of Aressotle for nothing. If Vhyl admired it, then he acquired it by any means necessary, and once he did, whatever he coveted disappeared into his well-guarded treasury, never to reappear again.

His mother was so proud of his accomplishments and his sister so jealous of his reputation. As for Vhyl, he knew he was on the path of fame and success given they both plotted his demise to inherit his fortune. What more could a male warrior ask for?

*Well, for starters, I could ask that the human bend over again.*

Arriving in a room lined with cabinetry and smelling pleasantly of chocolate—a delicacy he'd indulged in on more than one occasion, despite its high price at the Obsidian market—the female had briefly pushed her posterior in the air as she opened a hinged metal portal. A blast of heat wafted out, and Vhyl placed his hand on his sidearm, only to relax as she withdrew a flat metal sheet sporting brown-spotted blobs atop it.

She slid the tray on a countertop before turning to face him. Once more he got to study her intriguing features.

Skin the rich brown color of a Jkinja tree in bloom. It appeared silky and blemish free. He wondered if the rest of her flesh was covered with the same smoothness.

Unlike the males of her kind—which he'd familiarized himself with by briefly studying humans and their history on his way to this distant solar system—she didn't sport any facial hair, but the crown of her head did spill an abundance of dark locks. Curly and springy hair that he could easily imagine digging his fingers into as she knelt presenting her padded posterior. With buttocks like that, she was made to cradle a male's thrusts. And, yes, they were sexually compatible, another thing he'd learned on his voyage over.

Lusciously full lips pressed tight together at his perusal while big brown eyes, light in color and flashing with suspicion, stared right back. A female with fire and a backbone.

His intrigue level rose a notch higher.

"Would you like a freshly baked cookie?" she asked, waving her hand at the unappetizing lumps with the dark spots.

"I am not here for your baked goods." It almost made him shudder to realize this world still cooked with raw ingredients. Everyone, except unenlightened barbarians, knew replicators were the only way to eat decent food.

"A shame, because they're really quite good. I use Grandma's secret recipe." Despite the heat radiating from the blobs, she grabbed one and blew on it.

Did she realize the sensuality in her gesture? Did she do it on purpose in an attempt to rouse him?

Whatever the case, it was working. It almost distracted him, but he'd trained well and managed to remain focused. He was also cognizant that she seemed a little too calm given the situation.

"You seem awfully composed. I was given to understand your kind is prone to fits of hysteria, especially when faced with strange phenomena." And he knew enough of her world to understand his arrival and presence fit in that category.

She shrugged as she bit into the blob, a rumble of content purring forth from her. Whereas before he might have rebuffed her offer, he now found himself interested in a taste—from the lips where a drop of chocolate lingered. The tip of a pink tongue emerged to clean it, and he could have groaned.

She really seemed determined to rouse his lust.

"Panicking isn't going to do me any good. But I'll admit I would like to know who you are. Or should I ask, what are you?"

A request for information. Just how much could he tell her? Did he dare give her his real name? It wasn't as if she would recognize it, but at the same time, his self-imposed mission was supposed to be a secret, which begged the question, why did he land in front of her home and show himself to her? What happened to stealth?

For one, according to his vessel's readings, the artifact he was seeking hid inside this house.

So close. *Almost mine.*

Secondly, he'd caught a glimpse of her on his video stream during his approach and found himself intrigued by his first true glimpse of an earthling. A female one. A female who might have a clue that would lead him to the artifact and was still waiting for him to reply.

He stuck to the simplest answer he could think of. "I am an alien."

Given Earth had yet to join other planets in the galactic union, because they were considered little more than barbarians who had yet to achieve the right level of progress, he expected some shock on her part.

Wrong.

His declaration met with her sighing and rolling her eyes. "Duh. Any idiot with a pair of eyes can see you're not from this planet. So where are you from? Mars? Venus? The Milky Way? And what are you doing parking yourself on my front lawn? You're not some kind of vanguard to a larger army on a mission to conquer Earth?"

"No."

"Damn."

Odd how she seemed disappointed.

"Are you planning to kill me?" she inquired as took another bite of her concoction.

"Not at the moment. But that could change." Violence didn't bother Vhyl. Actually, he reveled in it. Chaos, too. He was the model son, or so his mother boasted to all her friends.

"Is it your intent to kidnap me?"

"For what?" He had no need of the money one of her kind would bring at auction. Nor did he have a use for organic attendants, not when he had all kinds of bots to do chores for him. *But I could use a new bedmate.* He'd broken his pleasure droid with

15

his vigorous technique, and there wasn't a clean bordello in this sector.

"I thought aliens were supposed to abduct us for probing experiments."

"If you insist on probing, I could indulge you, but it won't be an experiment, more an experience in pleasure." He showed his teeth in a pointed leer.

She snorted. "I see alien men are just as convinced of their prowess as human ones. Sorry to disappoint, but I'd prefer you kept it tucked in your jumpsuit. So if you're not here for murder, pillage, rape, or world domination, what does that leave?" She seemed genuinely puzzled.

She did raise some valid points. *Most of my missions involve mayhem of some kind.* In this case, unless she suddenly decided to use the gun she'd lowered, he'd simply have to find the treasure hidden in her home and depart. But he could hardly tell the female he was here to abscond with one of her possessions.

"I'm here for cultural education?" Even he couldn't help the querying note at his reply. As answers went, it wasn't his best, but what other reason would anyone have to visit this backwards world?

"You're here to check out Christmas?" Her nose wrinkled, and while on some species that would prove unattractive—such as the Balenjga tribe, who shriveled their nose before regurgitating for their young via their nostrils—in her case, her puzzled countenance proved most becoming.

Odd how his past studies of the barbarians

on Earth never properly conveyed how attractive some of them were. *Perhaps her suggestion of abduction and probing should make my list of things to do while planet-side.* Sure there were laws against meddling with humans. And, yes, it could cost him his life if caught or discovered.

Danger? Law breaking? Wild sex with a new species?

Things were looking more and more promising.

"Earth to freaky alien dude who still hasn't answered my question," she said, jolting him from his musings.

He frowned. It wasn't like him to be so easily distracted. "Yes, I am here on a mission to learn more about Kris-mass."

"It's Christmas, eh."

"Kris-mass, eh."

"No, Christmas. Say it slowly, with a hint of a t and less s at the end. Roll your tongue."

He'd roll his tongue all right and tie hers in a knot if she didn't stop vexing him. He'd pronounce it any damned way he pleased. He wasn't actually interested in any pagan holiday. "Don't make me revise my mission and change it to murder," he growled as he adopted a menacing mien.

To his shock, she giggled. "Ha. Nice try at scaring me. I grew up as the only girl with eleven boy cousins and a Grandma who believed in tough love. If that's your mean look, it needs work."

"Where I come from, females respect their males. Or else." He made sure to give her his ominous voice.

She ignored it. "Or else what?"

"They are punished." Although, honestly, he'd never seen or heard in what fashion. All he knew was his father would yell, his mother would sometimes yell back, they would stomp off and slam their bedroom door and not emerge for a long while. But when they did, his mother seemed properly chastised, or at least quiet, and his father boasted a grin.

She didn't seem impressed with his threat. "Touch me, purple dude, in a way I don't like and we'll have a problem."

"You really shouldn't be testing my patience this way. I've killed for less. Where I come from, my reputation alone is enough to make all but the most stalwart tremble."

"Your big, bad act might work on guys, but I'm not a guy, and I can see you're a softie. Anyone interested in Christmas isn't going to hurt a defenseless woman."

"Given you greeted me with a weapon, one could argue you aren't defenseless."

The smile curving her lips made her much too attractive. "I like to think of myself as prepared."

"Is your world so dangerous that you must have a weapon at all times? Where is your male? Your guardian? He should be here protecting you."

She outright snickered. "Sorry, oh misogynist one, there's just me." Too late she realized her admission and she sealed her lips shut.

His turn to smile. "All alone. Excellent."

"Not quite. I have my trusted friend, Problem Solver." She patted her projectile weapon.

"You gave that clunky artifact a name?"

"Don't tempt me to show you how efficient it is."

"Efficient is my sidearm." He pulled forth his favorite weapon.

Once again, he was treated to her laughter.

"That teeny tiny thing? Well, at least you're not trying to overcompensate for a lack of equipment elsewhere."

It took a moment for him to filter her meaning. "Are you implying I'm less than adequately endowed?"

A red hue brightened the cheeks of her face. "Um, no. I guess I shouldn't have said that."

"If you require a visual demonstration of my appendage, which given your earlier inquiry as to my intention to possibly probe you, then please, let me know. I will gladly clear up any misconceptions you might harbor about the size or virility of my reproductive system." The translator made his words emerge more properly than he would have liked. He really needed to upgrade to the newer slang version.

"You can keep your big dick to yourself. I'll take your word for it. Besides, I've no need of a lover."

"Lover? Who said anything about affection? Any demonstration of my virility would not involve emotion, just bodily satisfaction."

"Still not interested. Now can we get off the topic of sex and back on track?"

"If you insist. As I recall, we were discussing the fact that you have no guardian or mate." Not that it would have mattered. Vhyl had no issue with eliminating competition.

"Listen, purple dude—"

"My name is Vhyl." He chose to give her his shortened name. It wasn't as if she could do anything with it.

"Vile? Why am I not surprised? I'm Jilly, in case you care. Now, I don't know about where you come from, but on Earth, women don't need guardians. We are perfectly capable of taking care of ourselves."

How preposterous. "What of your defense?"

"Against what?"

"People like me." As he spoke, he moved, crossing the rectangular counter space that separated them. Landing on the other side, he smoothly plucked the weapon from her with one hand while the other wrapped around her curvy frame and drew her against him.

Her breath caught in a startled gasp, and her eyes widened as she stared at him. "Let me go."

"No."

She squirmed, to no avail against his greater strength, which, given her brows drew together, vexed her. "This isn't funny. Let me go at once."

"Are you making demands?"

"What if I said please?"

How sweet her lips looked when they

curved in a questioning plea. But they'd look better wrapped around a certain aroused part of his anatomy—only once he'd accomplished his quest. "I will release my grip and give you my word you will come to no harm if you tell me how to find the XiiX stone." Forget his earlier lie that claimed he visited for cultural education. Time to get his mission back on track so he could then indulge in pleasure.

"The what?"

"The XiiX? Don't play the innocent. According to the energy signatures my ship picked up, it is located somewhere within your abode."

Again, she wrinkled her nose, and he found himself fighting an urge to lean in a little closer and taste her lips.

"You're looking for some alien artifact?"

"Not just any artifact, the XiiX. It's been lost for millennia but recent discoveries of some ancient scrolls on a dead planet have allowed me to trace its movement to your world."

"And you think it's here, on my farm?"

"I don't think. I know it is. Lead me to it," he commanded…but she didn't obey.

"Sorry, Vile. I can't help you."

"You will if you wish to remain unharmed," he growled, tightening his grip.

How lovely she felt in his grasp. Curvy, warm, and her scent? He could fetch a fortune for it if he could bottle it. Then again, that would mean sharing it, and Vhyl wasn't into that.

"You can stop with the threats. I would give

it to you if I knew what the hell you were talking about. What's it look like?"

Good question. All the ancient texts spoke about the XiiX, but none ever displayed any images. All he knew was it was made of Arcanius, one of the rarest metals in the known universe, which was how he was able to pinpoint the location in the first place. The energy signature was quite distinctive if you could calibrate the computers well enough to detect it. He'd killed the technician who'd programmed his.

"An actual description might prove difficult." As difficult as staying focused on his task rather than getting distracted by the scent of her. Her delicate aroma surrounded him in a sensual perfume that clouded his senses.

"Let me get this straight, you're looking for a treasure but you don't even know what it looks like?" She laughed, the act shaking the frame he still held hugged to his chest.

Given her closeness seemed to be affecting the blood flow to his brain and impairing his mental capacity, he let her loose and moved away. "Don't mock me, female."

"I'm not, just remarking on the impossibility of your request. If you don't know what we're looking for, then how can I give it to you?"

Blasted female. Like his sister, she used logic as her weapon. "I have a device that will ease the task by reading the molecular buildup and energy signature of the items in your home."

"Well then, why didn't you say so? What are

you waiting for to use it? Let's find this thing and get you on your way."

"Are you so eager for me to leave?" The concept that she wanted to rid herself quickly of him didn't sit well. Most females begged him to stay. He had more than one reputation in the universe, and the other made him a prize among the opposite gender.

"No offense, but I've got more important things to worry about than your stupid treasure."

"I highly doubt that. I've come to the conclusion that the universe does revolve around me and has for some time. It's what happens to those who accomplish great things."

"I'm surprised your ego fits through the door."

"If it didn't, I'd blow it up," was his reply. He smiled at her taken-aback expression.

"Isn't that a bit extreme?"

"A male does what he can to attain notice. And even better if it involves violence."

"Grandma would have loved you," was her odd muttered reply.

He chose to ignore it. He had more pressing needs. "Given time is of essence," lest his competition appear and attempt to steal the XiiX from under him, "I will send my surface pod to my ship to fetch the tracking device."

"Aren't you just like a man to forget to pack the crucial things?" she muttered.

And wasn't she just like a woman to know how to say just the right thing to take a male down a peg?

He frowned, sternly, an expression that had sent more than one lesser being scurrying to do his bidding, eager to please him. By all the moons circling the ocean world in the seventy-first quadrant, that very look had seen him gifted with riches, fathers offering up their daughters, some beings even flung themselves from parapets, overcome by fear.

The human barbarian, though?

She ignored him and moved through an archway into another room.

Being a magnanimous male, he allowed it. It wasn't her fault her feeble barbarian mind couldn't handle his greatness and sought relief by removing herself from his presence in an effort to compose herself.

Tapping into the control unit at his wrist, he programmed his capsule to return to his ship currently in orbit around the Earth's moon. It was positioned out of sight, hovering under a cloak of invisibility on the dark side of the satellite where human detection units were blind.

Since it would take a while for his pod to fetch the detection unit and return, he went looking for the feisty human who seemed to think she was in charge of the situation.

*Time to disabuse her of that notion.* And maybe get started on more pleasurable things while he waited.

# Chapter Three

*"If a man is too good looking to be true, then he's probably a mass murderer. So keep him away from the kitchen knives." – Grandma's philosophy on handsome men.*

Jilly left the kitchen for more than one reason. The first to give herself some distance from the purple invader. Secondly, because she *really* needed some distance from the alien male in her house.

Okay, so the reasons were the same. Who could blame her?

Just look at him.

Distracting. Sexy. Obviously dangerous. Possibly deranged.

This Vile individual definitely didn't conform to any preconceived notion she'd ever held about what life out there might entail.

For one thing, he was much more human than she liked. Oh, sure he sported purple skin, black lips, and freaky pointed teeth, but the rest of him?

Good grief, the rest of him was straight out of some male stripper fantasy. The snug coveralls he wore did little to hide his excellent musculature. Broad shoulders, tapered waist, corded thighs, bulging arms… he was the epitome of male fitness with a face to die for, if you were into purple alien dudes who seemed to think women were useless creatures in need of a man to protect them.

Grandma would have shot him for that foolishness alone.

Thing was, Jilly didn't want to shoot him. On the contrary, she'd obviously gone too long between boyfriends because, silly her, she wanted to run her hands over the broad planes of his chest and invite him to show her his supposedly impressive package.

Crazy. As crazy as him showing up at her farm looking for some so-called priceless artifact.

What could it be?

Jilly knew every item in this house. She'd grown up here after her ditz of a mother dumped her more than twenty-seven years ago.

Raising a kid wasn't on her mother's to-do list. It clashed with the drugs and partying that came from being a music groupie. Thankfully, Jilly had her grandma to take up the slack.

Jilly never wanted for anything growing up. Grandma and Grandpa gave her everything she ever needed—a home, an education, clothing, affection, a sense of pride in herself, a quirky philosophy on life, and an ability to face any situation.

Even alien ones.

Grandma had also willed the farm, the house, and all its contents to her only granddaughter stating that her other cousins, all boys, could suck it up and get a job.

So when Grandma succumbed to that 'pesky cold' at the age of eighty-three, Jilly inherited it all.

Apparently more than she knew.

*What on Earth could this XüX thing be?*

Was it a rock? Some kind of statue? Jewelry? She didn't have much of that.

As she wandered from the kitchen back to the living room—which Vile had vacated—she stared out the window at the still softly falling snow. She noted the space coffin no longer sat in front of her porch. Had Vile left with it?

A shiver down her spine warned her someone entered the room, an electric tingle of her senses, which let her know her purple guest had stuck around.

And he wasn't one to respect personal boundaries.

He pressed in against her back, a large, menacing, yet arousing presence, that made her heart flutter and her nipples tighten.

"Do you mind?" she said a tad breathlessly.

"Mind what?"

She couldn't help but tense as her entire body woke, aware of Vile in a way she'd never before experienced. "You're standing too close."

"And?"

"And it's rude." But, most of all, arousing.

"Manners are for the weak," he stated, inching closer.

She fought not to gasp as his body brushed against hers. "Says who?"

"Says the handbook on mercenary rules that all my kind follow."

His race had a book on behaving badly?

"On Earth, it's considered disrespectful to ignore someone's personal space."

"Excellent."

"Excuse me?"

"I would hate to think I was tarnishing my reputation."

"You want to be known as a disrespecting jerk?"

"I prefer the title rule breaker."

"Well, break the rules somewhere else. You're making me uncomfortable." And hot. Much too hot.

"Uncomfortable or aroused? I think you protest because you enjoy my presence too much. So, no. I won't move away."

"Because you like annoying me?"

"No, because I'm enjoying the feel of you against me."

His surprising claim froze her tongue.

"What? No reply?" He chuckled and leaned in even closer, nudging her hair, sending shivers spiking down her spine.

This had gone on long enough. If he wouldn't move, then she would.

Or not. He slid an arm around her waist, anchoring her against him. He pushed aside the hair covering her ears, and his lips whispered against the lobe, increasing her awareness of him. "I am beginning to think there is more than one treasure in this house."

Her breath caught at the unexpected compliment. "I'm not an object."

"Perhaps not, but you are definitely something of worth. I am always looking to add to my collection."

"You can't just take me."

He laughed, the husky rumble somehow arousing, arousing enough that her sex moistened. Unbidden, her eyes closed, and she relaxed against him, mesmerized and curious about where this was going despite herself.

While a part of her—that sounded remarkably like Grandma—shouted at her to get away, another part basked in the male attention.

What woman didn't want to feel desirable?

What woman could truly say she didn't enjoy having such a virile male, one who admitted he came from a wider galaxy, think her attractive?

"Don't challenge me, female. I have a reputation for taking what I want, and right now, I want…" He trailed off, and she held her breath as she waited for his next words. "To know who the frukx is in those vehicles arriving."

Her eyes shot open, and she peered outside to see that indeed two large trucks, Suburbans to be exact, black in color with tinted windows, had pulled into her driveway.

"Who did you contact? Why are they here?" His grip went from sensual to tight and unrelenting as he hammered her with suspicious questions.

"I didn't call anyone. But if I had to guess, those are the feds. Not surprising really. I mean you weren't exactly subtle about your arrival."

"They are your planet guardians?"

She shrugged. "More or less."

"I do not wish to deal with them. The less who know of my presence, the better."

"Then you might want to hide because I have a feeling they're going to want to come in."

"Get rid of them."

"I intend to try. Trust me, I'm not any keener than you are about dealing with the government. Besides, even if you are a chauvinist with an ego the size of Kansas, you deserve better than getting buried in some government lab for experimentation and dissection."

"And it is for reasons such as these your planet is still considered so barbarian," he muttered. "Even though there is little honor in it, or fun, I will conceal myself, but do not think to betray me. It won't go well if you do."

With that ominous warning, Vile left her side, and Jilly took a deep breath before going to answer the pounding at her door.

For a moment, she debated fetching her gun, but vetoed it. Last thing she needed was to appear menacing. Best she find out what they wanted—probably a certain alien hiding out in her house—convince them she knew nothing, and send them on their way.

She opened the door and was faced with a trio of men in black suits, but, unlike a certain movie, they didn't wear sunglasses. Good thing, else, given the time of night, she might have been tempted to sing a certain Corey Hart song.

"Gentlemen, can I help you? Are you lost?"

The craggy fellow in the middle, his hair cut short and graying at the temples, perused her as he said, "Ma'am, I'm Agent Farley, and I'm here on behalf of the Department of Defense. We've come to check on a report of an unidentified object landing in this vicinity."

She widened her eyes. "Really? What was it? A meteor? Plane? Weather balloon?"

Agent Farley frowned. "No. Unidentified as in UFO, ma'am."

"Aliens?" She added a giggle to her faked incredulous reply. "You can't be serious. Is this some kind of a joke?"

"No joke, ma'am. Our equipment tracked an object to this location. Did you hear or see anything out of the ordinary?"

She shook her head. "Nope. I've been here all night, baking cookies. I haven't seen or heard a thing."

"Do you mind if we come in and look around?"

"Do you have a warrant?"

"We don't need one when it comes to the nation's defense."

"And how do I know you are who you say you are? I mean, anyone can put on a suit and claim they work for the government." She held the door only partially ajar as she refused them entry.

As if expecting this, badges were flashed at her, which again didn't prove anything. Jilly wouldn't know a real one from a fake one.

"Do you have a phone number I could call?

You know, so I can check on you."

"Ma'am, we are going to request you move away from the door."

"Or?"

"Please don't make this any more difficult than it needs to be."

"But I've already told you I didn't see anything. Your computers were wrong. So I don't see why you need to come in."

Agent Farley, who seemed to be in charge, addressed his next words to the guys who'd spilled out of the second suburban and approached.

"Take the woman into custody and then search this place."

"Hold on a second," she protested as they advanced on her, three men dressed in black combat gear replete with helmets and holstered weapons. Shit was starting to get uncomfortably serious and tense.

"Is there a problem?"

Vile's sudden question from behind her had her almost groaning. So much for bluffing her way out. Agent Farley would take one peek at his purple face and the jig would end.

Except the guys in front of her didn't react, but they did halt as Agent Farley said, "Who are you?"

An arm slid around her waist as Vile replied. "Her mate of course. My name is John. John Smith."

The most banal name in existence, which matched his totally banal human appearance.

Having peeked at Vile when he replied, Jilly had to consciously remind herself to not let her jaw drop as her previously purple, fanged visitor now sported Caucasian skin, normal, flat-edged teeth, and what appeared to be a plain white T-shirt and jeans.

Odd because pressed against him, her hand clearly touched fabric that was not denim-like in texture.

"The file we compiled on the way over made no mention of a boyfriend," said the government honcho with suspicion.

"I didn't know big brother was interested in my love life," she retorted, quickly recovering from her shock and doing her best to play along.

Not that it mattered.

"Grab him too," Agent Farley ordered.

"I would advise against it," Vile/John replied in a low voice at odds with the genial expression on his face.

"Now listen here, you are going to let us in so we can search the premises."

"But we have nothing to hide," Vile practically purred the words.

"We'll make our decision on that. Move aside. We need to—"

"Leave and report to your superiors you found nothing suspicious." Again, the words flowed from Vile in a silky torrent that made her shiver.

"We found nothing suspicious," the men, all six of them on her porch, repeated in a freaky monotone.

"You investigated the premises, questioned its occupant, and are satisfied she is hiding nothing."

"Hiding nothing," they aped.

"Leave now."

As if possessed of one mind, the men turned on their heels and marched back to their trucks. In moments, they had turned around and all she could spot were their taillights in the distance.

They'd left?

Just like that.

Impossible.

"Holy shit. What the hell did you do to them?"

"I reasoned with them."

"That was more than reasoning. It's like you hypnotized them."

"Perhaps. But it won't last." With that ominous announcement, Vile relinquished his grip on her and disappeared into her house.

Gaping at the now empty drive, Jilly took a moment to calm herself.

She tried counting.

*Oh my god, the feds were here. But Vile took care of them.*

Nails dug into her palms.

*He messed with the minds of government agents. That is bad. So bad.*

Irritation simmered. Reminding herself that anger accomplished nothing didn't help, especially since Grandma had raised her. Was it any wonder she couldn't stem the explosion?

# Chapter Four

*Collector rule number two. "Let nothing, especially not morals, stand in the way of you and your needed treasure."*

"What the hell do you mean it's temporary?"

The human female didn't quite yell at him, but her tone was not docile, or soft. Nor was her expression at all happy.

"Mental manipulation is only a short-term tool. Eventually, those with any kind of intelligence will realize they've been tampered with and override the commands."

"So that means those dudes will find out you screwed with them, and come back."

"Probably, but by then I should be long gone."

"Well la-di-da for you. What about me?"

"What about you?"

"Are you truly so self-centered? That's great that you get to walk away, or should I say zoom off in your flying saucer, but I still have to live here. I'd prefer to do so in my house and not behind bars."

"They would incarcerate you, a female, for what? Merely being here?"

"For being an accomplice to whatever it is you did to them. For lying about you even being here. For everything."

He made a moue of distaste. "Barbarians.

Only female criminals who've done truly heinous things are ever placed in prison. The ratio of males to females in the galaxy is too great for us to punish them at any length."

"Well, on Earth, if you do the crime, you do the time, and they don't care if you swing a dick or not. Fuck." She turned away from Vhyl and paced before a garishly decorated tree, which was, to his shock, not in a proper pot with soil but cut!

"What is that?" he said, pointing to it.

"It's a Christmas tree. And don't try to change the subject. Because of you, I'm going to be in deep shit."

"I see it's a tree, but it's been severed from its roots. Why would you do that?"

She frowned at him. "Because how else would I decorate it?"

"How about by transplanting it first? Or, even better, decorating it where it grew?"

"The guy with no morals is getting pissy over me cutting a tree. Oh, get over it. Thousands of people do it every year. It's tradition."

The shock of her admission almost made him gasp. Barbaric! "It's tradition to kill your plant life?"

"Not kill. Okay, so maybe the tree dies, but it is part of the holiday. And the tree farms plant new ones to take their place. Did you not study our planet at all before just deciding to drop in?"

What he did when going on a mission was known as reconnoitering, never something so emasculating as study. He arched a brow. "Studying is for scholars, not warriors."

"Hence your ignorance. You know, being smart doesn't make you a dumb warrior."

"It's a waste of time that could be spent practicing my skills or indulging in debauchery. Now stop diverting the topic away from yet another sign of your unenlightened nature. I do not grasp why you would massacre a tree and do this…" He gesticulated to the gaudy items hanging from the branches.

"We do it because it's pretty. See?" She leaned over, presenting her luscious backside and, for a moment, easing his incredulity.

The tree lit with dozens of small lights. It made the ornaments twinkle.

She stood back and a pleased expression crossed her face as she stared at the garish display.

He angled his head, left then right. "I fail to grasp the appeal."

"Your loss. I think it's pretty. Although it would be even prettier with a giant mound of cash sitting underneath."

Before Vhyl could reply, a golden glint caught his eye. He leaned closer and grasped a dangling disk, etched with symbols and hung on a branch with a red ribbon. "What is this?"

"A decoration."

Not given how it made his fingers tingle. "No. It's not." He plucked it from the tree and held it aloft, spinning it so it caught the light. "If I am correct, this is the XiiX."

"That ugly thing? Grandma says Grandpa

gave it to her, claimed it was some ancient Mayan treasure he picked up when he was in the army…" As Jilly spoke, her voice trailed off. "Holy crap. I guess that could be it."

"I will require my detection device to make certain, but given it emits a certain hum, I'd say it was a foregone conclusion."

"And mine." She plucked it from his grasp and tucked it against her protectively.

"A moment ago, you declared it was ugly."

"It is. Very much so. But it's still mine. So if you want it. Cough up."

"You wish me to expel air?"

She rolled her eyes. "It's an expression. Forget it. What I meant is how much are you going to pay me for it?"

Pay? Did she jest? Judging by her countenance, no.

He humored her. "What type of currency do you accept? Ghurian gems, galactic credits. I've got a cargo full of goods you can choose from."

She shook her head with each suggestion. "None of those are going to work. My bank only understands one thing. Cold, hard cash. If you want this XiiX thing, then you're going to have to pay me for it in American dollars."

"Or I can just take it." He reached over to grab it, but she hid it behind her back and shook her head.

"No way. The least you can do since you're going to be the possible cause for a lot of grief is compensate me properly for it."

"How about I pay you in pleasure?" He smiled.

She laughed. "If I need an orgasm, I'll touch myself."

The statement shocked him. "A female shouldn't masturbate, especially if a male proves willing to ease her arousal."

"Dude, just how repressed are the women in your world?"

Honestly, he wouldn't know. He didn't pay much attention to the females in his household, and his bedmates were just that, bedmates. Nothing more.

But perhaps he should revise his stance. He'd never before had such a stimulating time with a member of the opposite sex, at least one that wasn't related to him.

The fact he'd found a woman unafraid to defy him and, at the same time, aroused him was a heady combination. Unfortunately, she didn't seem to share the same intrigue.

*She rejected me!*

Vhyl, turned down by a female?

The universe that revolved around him ground to a halt. He needed to regain control.

*I could kill her and take the artifact.* But only cowards killed females, and Vhyl was renowned for his bravery. Surely he wasn't about to let a female, and a barbarian one at that, best him.

So if he didn't kill her, what option did that leave? *With my strength, I could just take the XiiX, and she couldn't stop me.* He could, but again, it didn't seem sporting. He was easily the stronger, faster, and more aggressive of them. Not to mention she might get hurt and, for some reason, that bothered him.

*What about seduction?*

She had said no, more than once, and claimed herself immune to his charms, but, after having observed her in a few different scenarios now, Vhyl had to wonder.

Perhaps she lied. Perhaps she did feel some of the same arousal as him but sought to deny it. A perverse characteristic of her kind perhaps.

Only one way to find out.

Since she'd tucked her hands behind her back, she could do nothing to stop him when he invaded her space with a few quick steps and wrapped his arms around her.

"What are you doing?"

"Taking." Although he couldn't have said what exactly he took—advantage of the lips, which parted as she gasped, or the ornament he could feel clasped in her hands?

The kiss stole any thought but one. *More.*

The taste of her proved exotic. Intoxicating. He might not have much experience in lip meshing—most sexbots didn't invite that kind of intimacy, and his bedmates often weren't of the most pristine sort, so he tended to avoid such contact—but with Jilly?

Luscious Jilly not only made him crave a taste, he wanted more. He plundered her mouth, leaving no part of it untouched. He took advantage of her parted lips to glide his tongue in and engage in a wet duel with hers.

He kissed her deeply, passionately, and hungrily, a male starving.

Despite her previous protests, Jilly did not fight him. On the contrary, her hands crept up his chest and draped around his neck, the warm metal of the artifact clasped in her fist pressed against him as she clung to them both.

To his delight, she didn't remain passive in his arms. She was an active player in their embrace, greedily sucking at his lower lip when her tongue wasn't engaging his.

Her aggressive takeover of the kiss both shocked and delighted him.

A female wanting control of the tryst?

A first for him. While females often invited him to their bed, once there, he did all the work. Did it well, too. And he found his pleasure, just as he gave them pleasure.

But to have a female so fervently throw herself into a kiss? To have her press herself against him, her lush body molding to his, her panting hot breaths and racing heart an indication of her ardent desire?

Vhyl was well and truly intrigued—and immensely aroused.

His hands roamed her body, cupping the fullness of her bottom, squeezing, weighing. Their roundness would prove inviting when he took her from behind and pounded into her flesh, but only once he got rid of their latest round of visitors.

With a loud curse, he pulled from the kiss as

a bright light shone through the window.

He wasn't alone in his disappointment.

"Dammit. They're back already," she grumbled.

"No. This company is worse than anything your government or planet could send against us."

"What do you mean?" she asked.

Her house began to shake.

"What the hell?" Fear widened her gaze as her home trembled. From outside, he could hear the rumble of anti-impact thrusters as a vessel came in for a less-than-subtle landing.

"We need to leave," he announced.

"Why? Who's coming?"

"My enemy," was his ominous reply.

# Chapter Five

*"If ever the farm comes under attack, don't forget I keep extra shot gun shells in the front hall candy bowl and a few spare guns in the trunk in the attic." – Grandma's philosophy on always being ready.*

Lips tingling, pulse racing, Jilly initially thought the shaking under her feet was passion induced, until his words penetrated.

"What do you mean it's your enemy?"

However, Vile wasn't answering. Instead, he tugged her away from the window and twirled her so her back faced it. Just in time, too.

Glass shattered as a wave of force smashed into them. The impact sent her to her knees, and she grunted, mostly because a giant purple dude threw his body around hers, forming a protective cocoon. Good thing given the tinkling shower of shards that blasted past them.

When the house stopped moving and the only thing they could hear was the rumble of the alien craft outside, he rose and yanked her to her feet.

"I can see why they outlawed that ancient thruster design," Vile complained.

While Jilly had emerged mostly unscathed, she noted her alien shield hadn't. Dark blood dripped from his left hand, and glints of glass sparkled in his hair. "You're worried about their engines? What about the damage? And I don't just mean to you."

The carnage around her—from the knocked over Christmas tree to the overturned furniture and shredded drapes—would have sent a normal woman fleeing in terror. It only served to piss Jilly off.

As Vile, a hand in the middle of her back, propelled her from the destroyed living room to her kitchen, which had fared only slight better with its broken windows, Jilly uttered a nasty curse word.

"Exactly how," he asked in a conversational tone, "is encouraging my enemy to fornicate with thy mother an appropriate response to this situation?"

It took her a moment to once again realize that modern slang wasn't part of his handy-dandy translation gadget. "Think of the nastiest thing you can call a person. What I just said is the Earth equivalent," was her retort.

"Noted. Even if I don't grasp it. Of more import than your odd Earth sayings, do you still have the artifact?" he asked as he peered through a window into her backyard.

Surprisingly enough, she did, clenched in her fist. "I do."

"Excellent. In that case, we will vacate the premises while my enemy is disembarking. The gravity on your planet will give us somewhat of a lead. Do you have a terrain vehicle at your disposal or one nearby we can acquire?"

"No need to steal a car. My truck's parked

out back by the barn. You can borrow it and run if you want, but I'm not leaving." This was her land. If these space invaders thought they could just bust up her farm, then they had another thing coming. Like Hell was she letting them get away with it.

Was facing down someone Vile recommended running from bright? Probably not, but Jilly had too much of her grandma in her to flee without a fight.

Jilly snagged her shotgun from the floor where it had been knocked over. She checked the chambers to ensure they were loaded. She also swapped her bunny slippers for the boots by her back door and shrugged on a coat. If she was going alien varmint hunting, then she'd probably want to make sure she didn't lose any body parts to frostbite in the attempt.

"Your weapon won't prove effective against the one coming," he informed her.

"How can you know? You've never seen me use it." It punched a decent sized hole.

"Unless it spits high temperature flames or an extremely corrosive acid, then projectiles will just pass through its gelatinous mass."

"Jelly? Your enemy is made of jelly?" She tried to imagine what such a creature would look like as Vile dragged her out the back door.

He grabbed her free hand as he ran from the farmhouse, his long stride forcing her to huff and puff to keep up. The barn loomed in the distance, a ramshackle structure that hadn't seen use in at least a decade. Jilly kept waiting for a strong wind to blow it down.

Parked about a dozen feet from the barn doors was her vintage, 1980's Dodge Ram pickup truck. Diesel of course. It chugged, blew smoke, and was anything but discreet, yet it did the job getting her around. When it started.

Given her remote location, and the fact she kept hoping someone would steal it, she always left the keys in the ignition, which proved handy right about now given their need for a hasty getaway.

As Vile made a beeline for the driver's seat, she barked, "I don't think so, purple dude."

"I am a renowned combat fighter who has driven vehicles through some of the harshest conditions. I'll program our escape route."

Confident words, which he soon ate.

He slid into the driver's seat and stared at her dashboard in consternation. "What the frukx is this archaic technology? There is a circle on your dash. Where is your control panel? Your keypad for programming coordinates?"

"It's called a steering wheel and if you don't know that this thing is driven by the pedals on the floor, then you need to move your ass over."

To her surprise, he didn't argue. He slid over the bench seat to the passenger side. She hopped in, gun first, which he snagged from her and placed between his knees.

Jilly didn't waste time. She turned the key in the ignition and muttered her standard magical chant. "Come on, baby. Start for me. Let's go. Mama needs to get her butt moving."

"What are you doing?"

"Praying to the gods of trucks and automobiles that my baby here," with over a million miles clocked and still ticking, most days, "will start." She slapped the steering wheel and pumped the gas a few times to prime the carbureted engine. "Come on, you big bastard. Start."

*Chug. Chug. Rumble. Gasp. Choke.*

"Is that sound normal?" he asked.

"Depends on your definition of normal. My truck sometimes has a bit of a temper when it comes to starting."

"This is not a good time for it to get angry. We need to get moving. Things are about to get hot."

"Things are about to get slapped if they don't shut up and let a girl do what needs to be done," she muttered.

"Duck!"

Before she could ask why, he was shoving her head down, just in time, too, as a massive explosion rocked her vehicle. Something hard hit the windshield, and when Vile allowed her to raise her head, she blinked at the smoldering shoe on her hood.

*That's my shoe.* Which she'd last seen in her bedroom closet on the second floor of her house.

Slowly her gaze rose, and in her side mirror, she caught sight of a red/orange flicker before the acrid stench of smoke hit her nose. She turned her head and gasped. "My house!"

More like her ruin.

Her home, the place she called her own—or would have until the bank took it away—no longer existed. A smoldering ruin sat in its place, the jagged remains made of century-plus old wood dancing with flames while black smoke billowed into the sky.

"That bastard blew up my house!" Shocked, she turned to Vile and yelled. "This is your fault!"

"How is it my fault? I am sitting right beside you. You should be thanking me."

"Thanking you for what?"

"If it weren't for me, you'd have been inside. And," he said with pursed lips as he perused her, "you would have probably died given your fragile nature."

"Oh, that's priceless," she snarled. "Blame the victim. This happened because of you and that stupid artifact. It's your fault your jelly friend—"

"Enemy," he corrected.

"—followed you here and destroyed my house."

"He will also destroy us if you don't move this vehicle. If I am not mistaken, which I rarely am, Mo is approaching."

That claim managed to stem her tirade as she drew her gaze away from Vile and focused it outside. Sure enough, coming down the drive, waving tentacles, some of which held what she could only surmise were weapons, was an honest-to-goodness jellyfish on land.

"Holy fuck." She breathed the expletive as she wrenched the key one last time and jammed her foot on the gas.

*Chugga. Chugga. Vroom*!

This time the engine caught and held, its noisy motor revving high. She took her foot off the brake, slammed the truck into first, and the truck lurched forward.

So did Vile's head, but he managed to brace a hand on the dash and prevent a concussion.

"You might want to buckle up," she advised, having already drawn her own seatbelt automatically upon getting in.

Being a male, he, of course, ignored her to instead point out the obvious. "You're heading right for him," Vile yelled over the rumble of the engine.

"Yup." Forward was the only way out of her farm. The fields at their back only went for a few acres before the land dipped sharply into an impassable ravine.

"Are you insane? He's aiming his weapon at us. You'll get yourself killed."

"You'll die, too, if you don't use that teeny tiny thing you call a gun to distract him."

"Actually, my jumpsuit will protect me from most impact."

"Stop being a smug jerk and shoot," she hollered as she floored the gas and weaved her way towards the tentacled shape, which had stopped moving and now appeared to be taking aim.

"Bossy barbarian," he muttered. Despite his complaint, he took aim, and shot—right through her windshield.

Dammit!

But she couldn't really give him too much

hell since the beam of light, which punched a neat hole through her windshield, streaked ahead of them, hit Jelly dude, and sliced a limb clear off. Stroke of luck or on purpose, it happened to be the one with a weapon pointed at them.

She slapped the steering wheel. "Woo!" she crowed. "Nice shot."

An unearthly—and she meant that quite literally—squeal erupted, and the remaining tentacles waved wildly. Jilly flashed Mo—which had to be the universe's stupidest name for an alien— the bird as she flew by in her rattling truck.

Energized by their small victory, she exclaimed, "Dude, we should stop and turn around. I take back all the nasty things I said about your little gun. It's amazing. Do it again." Maybe they wouldn't have to flee after all. Vile could just keep shooting the other alien dude until it had no waggling arms left.

"That wouldn't be advisable," was Vile's dry reply. "There is a reason we advocate strong flame or acid when dealing with Mo and his kind."

Peeking into her rearview mirror, Jilly's eyes widened, and her mouth closed on her "Why?" as the severed limb on the ground jumped.

And wiggled.

And rippled.

Why, it jiggled itself into a second mini jelly dude.

"What. The. Hell!"

"Congratulations. You've just seen the birth of a new Gelabli. Now do you see why I advocated we flee?"

"That's insane."

"No. It's how they reproduce."

Startling and disturbing. "Wow, given how easily they can multiply, have they like taken over the galaxy?"

"They've tried. However, given we know their weakness, they had to give up. Also, they are covetous and violent by nature, even with their own progeny. To lose a part of themselves means weakening until they can ingest enough material to regain what they've lost. And since they don't like to share, many younglings don't survive."

"That is seriously messed up," she muttered as she careened down the rest of her long driveway and fishtailed onto the country road. In the rearview mirror she could still see the glow of the fire consuming her home and see the dark cloud of smoke in the sky.

It hit her then.

*I'm homeless.*

The fact that she probably wouldn't have found the money for the bank before the bank's foreclosing date didn't hurt as much as knowing, even if she did encounter a miracle, she had no house to go back to.

Nothing. Just what she wore, her truck, and the stupid artifact she'd stuffed in her coat pocket.

It was a lot to take in. A part of her wanted to cry. A part of her wanted to rail at the injustice. A part of her…found it strangely exhilarating, which was why, instead of blasting Vile, she said, "What next, purple dude?"

# Chapter Six

*"It's not stealing if you manage to point out flaws in a security network." – How to justify your acquisition should the previous owner file a complaint.*

What next involved them finding somewhere to hole up while Vhyl checked on the status of his vessel. It perturbed him that his enemy had tracked him to Earth. His fault for using a pod craft instead of more stealthy means.

Of more concern than the Gelabli attack was the fact Vhyl now had to worry about the state of his spacecraft. Even though his vessel's cloaking was engaged, Mo might have located and sabotaged Vhyl's ship—which would really irritate Vhyl, as he'd only recently acquired the wondrous craft— straight from the government facility where they'd developed it in the Lojica Galaxy, a place renowned for their wondrous inventions but unwillingness to share them.

Since Vhyl didn't like their stance, he took it. In retaliation, they locked the vessel down, making him a prisoner on it until he agreed to their price tag—the annihilation of the solar system alongside them where their greatest competitors lived. While paying for something went against the mercenary way, destroying things didn't. Hence he paid their price.

Then he returned to Lojica for a few more toys he coveted. He considered the flaws he uncovered in their security system payment of a sort for the items he acquired. If you asked him, he'd done them a favor, and as such, the objects he took were compensation for a job well done. Given he was pointing a gun at their president at the time, they agreed on his generous price.

"I must contact my ship and arrange for transportation for myself and the artifact off planet. Therefore, we need a secure location where we might rest, wait, and plan."

"What's wrong with where you are now?" she asked.

'Now' had a spring digging in his backside, spewed fumes that were probably toxic, and was about as subtle as a Lxroakian charging through a glass shop. "I'd prefer something a little more comfortable. Does your planet not have establishments that allow visitors the use of rooms for short stays?

"Yeah, we have hotels and motels."

"Take us to one then. Preferably one in a civilized location. My enemy will have difficulty blending in, and despite his brazen attack at your farm, he won't want to draw unwanted attention to himself." Lest he bring the galactic police after him for breaking one of the council's iron-clad rules about planets that didn't belong to their consortium.

The rules revolving around uninitiated worlds, such as Earth, spanned several tomes of literature but boiled down to one simple phrase:

Stay away from Earth.

"Book us a room, he says." She snickered. "Good luck with that. I didn't have time to grab my wallet. Without money, there isn't a place in the world that will give us a room. The best I can do is park on the side of the road and hope the cops don't cruise by and cite us for loitering."

"I will handle any requests for finances. Just find us a hostelry."

"If you insist."

"I do."

As she drove, the occasional passing vehicle illuminating her features, Vhyl wondered that he still traveled with the barbarian female. More than that, he'd saved her. First from the government agents who would have taken her. Then from the explosion of glass and Mo's arrival. It would have astonished anyone who knew him that he hadn't ditched her to escape on his own.

*Frukx if I know why I'm still with her. Or why I keep defending her.*

This type of protective instinct went against his usual morals. By all the moons he'd destroyed— because he did so like to play with weapons of mass destruction—he'd never before wondered what it would be like to have a permanent bedmate in his life and a partner to share his career of mayhem and acquisitions.

What happened to enjoying his solitary life where the most important thing was the acquisition of rare goods?

It was lonely.

The revelation came to him suddenly and unexpectedly.

*I'm lonely.* The endless units of time where he did nothing but attempt to find something, anything to dull the boredom of travel. The moments when he accomplished something great and had no one but his mother to brag to.

Staring at Jilly's profile, he wondered what it would be like to keep her by his side, to have her welcome him after an exhilarating heist. To have her aid him in nefarious plots.

Insane. Where did these crazy ideas come from?

*It must be the oxygen levels of this planet rendering me irrational.* What else to explain it? He barely knew the female. *Other than the facts that she is fearless, outspoken, and tastes delicious.*

As the sun crested the horizon, Jilly pulled into a parking lot dotted with vehicles. A large sign flashed overhead, the A in Vacancies dark, but the meaning still quite clear.

"Now what, oh noticeable purple one?" she asked.

"Time to disguise myself and acquire the use of a room." Flashing her a smile, Vhyl tapped his wristband. With only a slight shimmer, he adopted a human glamour that would withstand close scrutiny, just not touch.

"Amazing," she murmured. "But I still don't know how you figure you'll get a key without a credit card or cash."

"Such doubt. You'll see." Vhyl wasn't a

master of acquisition for nothing.

In short order, he returned, bearing not only a key, but also an armful of culinary items to feed them both. Given his knowledge of this world, he was made to understand—to his dismay—that Earthlings had yet to manage proper food replication via a machine.

Utter barbarians. Growing their food and killing animals for consumption? That was something a warrior only did out of necessity. Civilized mercenaries and acquisition experts relied on technology to properly feed them.

Jilly was looking away from him when he emerged from the registration office, fingers tapping on the round thing she called a steering wheel, which, if he recalled his history lessons correctly, was something his kind had used on extremely early propulsion vehicles.

Shudder.

He much preferred the accuracy of a computer than relying on organic reflexes to guide him at high speeds.

He clambered into the truck, which even he had to admit had a certain rugged appeal. "The attendant placed us on the second floor at the far end," he told her.

"Second floor? Shouldn't we have taken the first for a quick escape?"

"Height is always an advantage," he informed her. "Much harder for assailants to surround when they must climb."

"Good to know. I'll store that with my other

bits of useless knowledge I'll never use again."

It took him a moment to grasp she jested, and to his surprise, he laughed. "Don't be so sure. Given your attitude, I am surprised you've led a strife-free life thus far."

"There is nothing wrong with my attitude."

"I didn't say I didn't appreciate your rapier wit. But, where I come from, a female with a saucy mouth like yours would definitely get in trouble."

Unless he was around. *I'd kill anyone who laid a hand on her. And enjoy it.*

"Well then, I guess it's a good thing I'm not a part of your world."

Not really. It surprised him to realize he'd probably miss their lively discourses once he departed.

"Ensure you park the vehicle facing outward in case we should require a hasty departure."

"What's wrong? Worried your coffin might not make it back in time to pick you up?"

Actually, yes. While he'd managed—despite the jostling of the truck—to ping his craft in orbit behind the moon, his transport carrier hadn't fared as well.

"My surface pod lost contact with my craft upon its return approach to your home."

"Jelly dude shot it down, did he?"

"No, it seems your military aerial defense intercepted it. I had to initiate a self-destruct sequence, lest it fall into their less-than-ready hands."

"No alien technology for us?"

"Your planet is on a non-tampering list."

"And yet here you are, tampering."

"Acquiring. There is a difference."

"So yours is sanctioned?"

"Of course not," he replied, unable to completely mask his indignation. "Perish the thought. My activities are completely illegal and punishable by death."

She regarded him with curiosity. "So why do it then?"

"What is life without a little danger?" His smile might have been a tad rakish. He did so find pleasure in breaking the law. But it seemed, in this instance, she found merit in his reaction because she returned his grin and laughed.

The sound, husky and genuine, thrilled him. He wanted to hear it again, but not out here in the open. "Let us get inside where we are less noticeable."

With his wrist monitor scanning the environs and his eyes also taking in the scenery, they made it to the second floor—using stairs of all things—and found their room, the first door, which Vhyl bypassed.

"What are you doing?" Jilly inquired. "I thought you said we had the end unit."

"We do. Which, if any enemies follow and question the attendant, is the first place they'll look. Hence why I stole this key while the clerk was otherwise occupied." A subtle suggestion to look away while Vhyl swapped the keys with a vacant one four doors away. Close enough to keep an eye on their supposed room but far enough to give them time and space to plot an escape if required.

He ushered them quickly inside.

The interior of their quarters proved less than impressive. Two less-than-sizable beds covered in a green patterned fabric, a single chair with a slick, almost plastic covering, and a view screen bolted to a piece of furniture with drawers.

Ugly, but serviceable.

He dumped the contents of his haul on the bed. Jilly eyed the stash and shook her head. "Holy junk food, purple dude. Chips and candy bars. So much for healthy."

"It was all the vending machine had."

She wrinkled her nose. "I guess beggars can't be choosers. It will be just like my good old college days when I used to live on chocolate bars and cola. With all that caffeine and sugar, at least I won't have to worry about falling asleep."

"You should take a moment to rest. We could be called upon to escape at any moment."

"What's with this 'we' stuff? You know, it occurs to me that most of my problems would disappear if I ditched you."

Yes, they probably would, and yet, he found himself reluctant to let her go. He tried to rationalize this strange feeling. "Given your association with me, you are probably safer at the moment in my company. My enemy might think you useful as a bargaining chip."

"Vile, is this your way of saying you care about me?"

"No. But they won't know that and might kill you in order to make me cooperate."

"Gee, don't I feel all warm and fuzzy inside."

"If it is of consolation, I would avenge your death."

"Not feeling any better."

"I know of something that would bring you great pleasure." And yes, he grinned widely to make his innuendo clear.

A reddish hue invaded her cheeks. A sign of her lust or something else?

"I think I'll pass."

"A pity."

"So, um, have you thought of a way to pay me for this?"

She plucked the artifact from a pocket and held it so it spun in the air. It glinted in the feeble light of a lamp, its low hum enticing, and yet, while he found the XiiX fascinating, it paled beside the woman who held it aloft. It confused him because for some reason he found himself questioning as to which was the greater prize—her or the XiiX?

Madness or the pollutants from her truck clouding his judgment?

The answer was clear. Or should be.

The XiiX was priceless. One of a kind, hence the race to acquire it. Well, not so much a race anymore, as it was technically in his possession, but until he managed to lock it away with his other treasures, someone could still come along and steal it.

And, yeah, he didn't see the irony in calling other collectors thieves. In his world, anyone who touched what was his was a thief.

*And if they touch Jilly?*

Then they would die. Because, more and more, he was beginning to think of her as his. Or at least worth keeping for a while to judge her worth.

If he bored of her, he could always kill or auction her off.

*As if I'd let another own her.* The very thought filled him with a cold rage.

*Mine.*

His.

He couldn't have said when he made the decision to kiss her again, or why. All he knew was one moment he was doubting his mental capacity, filled with a possessive need, and determined to touch her again.

He slanted his mouth over hers, and she tasted just as delicious as before. Perhaps even better. His arms wrapped around her, an embrace that tucked her against him, her shape, which he'd initially found so odd, fitting perfectly against his.

Given he'd set a perimeter defense—his wristband possessing a detection option that would inform him if it noticed weapons, certain distinct lifeforms or other out-of-place actions within a certain range—he felt rather safe in indulging. Then again, he would have indulged even without it.

Nothing like the threat of danger to make an encounter more exciting.

"We shouldn't be doing this," she managed

to utter between panting breaths.

"Why not?"

"Because I barely know you."

"Knowledge is a prerequisite for sex on your world?"

She paused in her nibbles of his lower lip to peruse him. "It's things like that comment that remind me you're an alien. That and the purple skin."

"And it's the fact you only have a pair of these," he said, squeezing each of her wondrous breasts, "that remind me you're human."

"I don't even want to know how many boobs your women usually have."

"It depends on their fecundity."

She blinked, and he could almost see her mind whirring, preparing a new round of queries.

Given the erotic moment appeared to be slipping away, he forestalled any further questions by placing his lips back upon hers while his hands did their best to massage her breasts. The nipples, which crowned them, hardened when he ran his thumb over the tips, peaking into hard buds that he could not resist.

Much as he delighted in the taste of her lips, he wanted to feel those peaks in his mouth. He wanted to suck on her and hear her moan in delight.

And she did.

Even though he initially grasped her erect tips through the fabric of her shirt, she not only moaned, she arched, and her fingers clasped his head, hugging him to her chest.

With a growl, he broke free. "Take off your shirt."

"Only if you take your...whatever you're wearing off as well."

Even in the midst of pleasure, she thought to negotiate. Lucky for her, her demand coincided with his own thoughts.

As she stripped off her shirt, baring her glorious breasts, he ran his fingers down the enclosure to his surface suit. It split apart, and he stepped from it, clad only in form-fitting shorts.

"Aliens wear underwear?" she asked, not without a lilt of surprise.

"I do. The suits can chafe a male's lower regions otherwise."

She laughed. "And it's comments like that that make you sound almost human."

He glared. "That wasn't nice."

"Oh, get over it," she scoffed as she kicked off her boots then tugged off her pants, baring her legs and the most delicious cocoa-colored thighs. Her own undergarments were made of just the tiniest scrap of fabric, and through their laciness, he could see the thatch that covered her mound.

He knelt between her spread limbs, determined to examine her more closely. Yet once again she showed her difference from other females he knew.

She wasn't content to lie back and let him explore. On the contrary, she seemed fascinated by him.

He sucked in a breath as she reached out to

touch him. "I don't know what's more fascinating, the fact you have no nipples or that you have the most lickable set of abs I've ever seen."

"What are abs?"

"These are." She raked nails down his flat stomach to the waistband of his shorts.

His cock swelled at her light, teasing touch. "My form pleases you?"

"Oh, it does, purple dude. Even if your lack of nipples is making me question my sanity in doing this, here and now."

"Live for the moment."

"Another of your mercenary rules?"

"That one is purely mine. No one can predict the future—even if those frukxing Lojicas claim they can. Part of my personal code is to take what I want when the opportunity presents itself, else you might lose that chance forever."

"Usually, I'd argue, but in this instance," once again she stroked his muscled belly, "you might have something. Come closer."

Curious at her intent, he leaned forward. She placed the palms of her hands against his pectorals.

"So smooth," she murmured.

It seemed only fair he return the favor, albeit one-handed given his other was needed to brace him lest he crush her. He cupped a breast, and she sucked in a breath at the contact.

"You are soft," he remarked. He squeezed the globe. "And squishy."

She laughed. "Whereas you," she dragged a hand low and rubbed against the front of his groin, "are not."

Leaning forward, he brushed his lips across the tip of her breast. Her whole body quivered.

"Do it again. But this time suck it," she demanded.

What a surprise, even during coitus she thought to keep control. He'd soon strip that habit from her.

He dipped his head lower and sucked on the erect nipple. She gasped then cried out as he bit down on the tip. He ran his tongue around the peak and then sucked at it again. Then repeated it on the other breast.

It pleased him to note she closed her eyes, obviously enjoying it. He grew bolder with her, less hesitant now that he knew she enjoyed some of the same sexual play he was familiar with. Even better, while he indulged in her responsive breasts, she touched him as well, her hands stroking over his upper chest, raking her nails on the sensitive skin.

Funny how such simple caresses could cause such an ardent reaction. His cock practically burst from its confines, determined to sink into her heat.

Vhyl alternated between pulling on her taut nipples with his lips and licking them. He gauged his progress by how heavily she panted and how hard she ground her mound, still covered in moist fabric, against his muscled thigh.

Kneeling on the bed, he stopped his decadent pleasuring of her buds to grasp her around the hips, all the better to help her rub against his leg. Whimpering cries escaped her as he placed pressure against her sex. A sex he suddenly wanted to see.

He tore the paltry lace that hid her from view. She didn't seem to mind. On the contrary, she begged. "Touch me."

Oh, he intended to. Arousal raged through his body, and were he more selfish, he would have just bared his cock and plunged into her welcoming sex. She was clearly ready. The lips of her mound glistened with moisture.

He knew from his studies of their kind, and rumors, that it was a common practice among humans to place kisses upon a woman's sex. But how would it taste?

Curiosity made him eager to know. He palmed her buttocks, lifting her to his mouth that he might find out. She groaned at his first tentative lick.

Sweet.

Musky.

And her reaction? A low groan, head thrashing, body quivering. He wanted more.

He stabbed his tongue into her, tasting the visible evidence of her arousal and, in return, felt his own need peaking.

"Yes. Yes. Yes," she chanted as she fisted the sheets, urging him on. As if he could stop now. His lips nudged a protrusion at the mouth of her sex, and she keened. Not just keened but bucked.

What was this? He located the nub with his tongue and stroked it.

She almost tore free of his grasp she reacted so violently, but not out of pain.

*By all the moons in the universe, I think I've found*

*her pleasure button.*

And now that he had, he exploited it. He circled his tongue around it, grasped it with his lips. He barely had time to play with it before she screamed his name and arched, her body bowing off the bed.

"Vile!"

Did his chest swell that she acknowledged him so vocally? Frukxing right he did. But at the same time, her obvious climax rendered him impatient to join her.

In order to ensure she remained amiable to more coital play, he kept licking at her pleasure button, quite enjoying her violent headshakes, her mumbled gasps, the trembling of her limbs.

When he could finally contain himself no longer, he yanked his remaining garment down enough to bare his throbbing cock. Lowering her to align her body with it, he couldn't help but growl, "Mine," as he plunged into her wet sheath.

The sensation proved mind shattering.

For the second time since meeting her, he could have sworn the universe slowed down in its revolution around his greatness. Time stood still. His shaft pulsed in the most welcoming haven he'd ever encountered.

When reality slammed back, Vhyl knew, somewhere in the back of his mind, that something had changed, but caught up in the rhythm of plunging his shaft in and out of her channel, he didn't bother to stop and analyze what.

All he knew in that moment was he'd never

felt anything more right.

More pleasurable.

More…

He came in a hot spurt just as her sex convulsed. She climaxed again, and her muscles clamped him tight, bringing him along with her.

He'd never felt anything more glorious.

Caught up in the moment, and not eager—for once—to see it end, Vhyl folded her tight to him, his arms wrapping around her upper torso as he rolled them both until he lay on his back, her atop him, still joined at the groin.

To his delight, she was the one who plundered his mouth, engaging him in a hungry kiss that stole what was left of his ragged breath. His fingers slid into her curly hair, anchoring her head, making sure the embrace would not end any time soon.

He didn't stop the groan that escaped him as her tongue slid between his lips. Had he ever enjoyed a more willing partner? One who made the most delightful sounds? As if to prove that point, she mewled into his mouth as he grazed pointed teeth along the length of her tongue.

Alas, while Vhyl was considered quite virile, even he required time to recuperate between sexual bouts. She didn't seem to mind.

Although she did sigh when they finally stopped kissing. "Would it be corny for me to say that was utterly out of this fucking world?"

"If you are implying that the experience was immensely gratifying, then I would have to agree."

"Since we're handing out compliments, your equipment did live up to its boast."

A grin quirked his lips. "I am a prime example of my kind. And then some."

She nipped his chin with her flat teeth. "But you are definitely not modest."

"Modesty is for the weak. In my culture, we take pride in ourselves."

"Speaking of culture, are all of your kind like you?"

"Physically, yes, although our actual height and weight might differ along with cranial hair coloring and eyes."

"I didn't mean looks-wise," she said with a laugh. "I mean attitude. You're so self-assured. Confident the world revolves around him."

"Universe," he corrected.

"See what I mean? You are so convinced of your superiority and seem unafraid of anything. I saw how you reacted when we were in danger. You didn't appear worried one bit."

"Danger is what warriors from Aressotle live for. We are raised to thrive on adrenaline filled moments. Weakness is shunned. Glory is everything. The most renowned warriors from my world are the universe's best assassins, mercenaries, and acquisition specialists."

"Sounds like you break a lot of laws."

"We prefer to think of ourselves as above them."

"What of the scholars and scientists? Surely you have those too."

"No male would ever bring such shame on his household. And if he tried, he would either be banished or killed."

"But I've seen some of your technology. If you don't create it, then how do you have it?"

He almost rolled his eyes at her question. "We take it of course. It is one of the earliest rules we are taught."

"But that's stealing."

"Only if you do it without finesse." He couldn't help but leer as he replied, and she laughed.

"So once you leave here, where to next? What grand adventure or pirating do you have planned?"

"Plan for the future? Perish the very idea. Have you already forgotten my motto of live for the moment? Or in this case," he waggled his hips as his cock revived itself, "live for the next climax."

It seemed she heartily approved, given she hungrily met his kiss and her sex squeezed him tight.

But despite their second round of stimulating play, he couldn't quite forget her question.

As they lay snuggled together—yet another new thing for him—with Jilly falling asleep—and not because he'd drugged her—he couldn't help for once imagining what he would do once he managed to get himself off-planet. Or the better question, would he leave this world alone?

# Chapter Seven

*"Regrets are for losers. Own up to your actions. After all, you're the one responsible for them."* – *Grandma's philosophy on life.*

*What have I done?*

Well, that part was obvious. Jilly had slept with an alien.

Okay, she didn't actually sleep, but they were in a bed.

Naked.

Limbs still entwined.

Her body still throbbing even hours later because Vile had shown her just how talented—and endowed—he truly was.

*Dammit, I think he might have ruined me for human men.*

Because either her lovers before were truly inept, or purple dudes from space truly did it better.

It surprised her to see his eyes closed, as if he slumbered. She would have expected him to keep watch, given his jelly enemy, Mo, was probably still looking for them.

Sleep however eluded her. The several-hour nap she'd nabbed after her second fabulous orgasm—her body shuddered in remembered pleasure—had left her feeling wide-awake.

She also felt quite sticky.

Taking care not to disturb him, she eased off

the mattress and went into the bathroom. Given she didn't know what would happen next, and the fact she was currently homeless, taking a shower seemed like the thing to do.

Of course, she could have done without the theme from *Psycho* running through her head as she stepped under the warm spray.

Comparing herself to one of those stupid women in movies who just had to bathe when danger lurked made her grimace. *At least now I can totally see why the girl in the haunted house has to get naked and take a shower.* It was probably because she'd just had sweaty sex and needed to sluice off.

Thinking about horror movies was probably why, when the curtain drew back, her first impulse was to scream. Loudly.

Vile grimaced. "Was that necessary?"

"You startled me."

"Apparently," was his dry reply. "Move over."

"Why?"

"Because I'm joining you."

Before she could protest the shower wasn't big enough, he proved it wasn't by getting in. Then again, there was an advantage to the tight confines. It meant he had to press his body against hers.

"I don't see how this will help us get clean," she said, surprised she sounded coherent, given her heart raced, her voice turned husky, and, much like a man, all her blood went south, making a certain part of her throb.

And to think she'd thought her greedy pussy

satisfied. It seemed all it took was a naked alien in her shower to forget the thorough pleasure he'd given her earlier.

"Who said anything about getting clean?" Vile asked as his arms came around her. "I joined you because you're naked. And wet. Which means you're slippery. I like slippery. Oh, and wet."

The way he said it, teasing, sexy, and yet utterly serious, just served to heighten her own arousal.

"Aren't you worried someone might sneak up on us if we're both in here?"

"For one, my detection field is still scanning for signs of danger, and two, did you not yet grasp that I thrive on danger?"

Given how she shivered, and her pussy melted, Jilly was beginning to wonder if she wasn't an adrenaline junky too.

It certainly did add that extra element to their sexual play to know, at any moment, someone could interrupt them.

"What are the chances Jelly will find us here?"

"If his archaic equipment has any kind of decent surface scanning equipment, then the probability is high. So we should probably not delay."

How his eyes practically glowed as he grinned and said it.

"We don't exactly have much room," she protested. A token protest of course. She was just as eager as him for another round.

"Turn around, and I'll make it work."

Or she could assuage her curiosity about alien equipment. Just in case she never got another chance. While she'd certainly experienced it, she had yet to truly see it.

Despite the tight dimensions of the shower, she managed to drop to her knees, bringing her eye-to-eye with his cock. His massive dark mauve cock and his...what the fuck?

"Dude, what happened to your sac?"

"Excuse me?"

"You have no balls." She lifted his shaft to peek underneath just to make sure they weren't tucked and hidden.

"Of course I don't."

"You mean this is normal? What is it, like some cultural thing where they remove them?"

He snorted, and it took her a moment to realize it was in mirth. "None of my kind have exterior hanging testes. Almost none of the evolutionized species do. A warrior's most precious gift to society, after his skills and prowess, is his ability to pass on his greatness. As if we'd risk having future generations of virile perfection exposed to injury."

While his explanation, on the one hand, served to showcase the difference between them, at the same time, it made him even more exotic than before. And besides, as she'd already learned, he didn't need any balls to bring her pleasure or perform.

But it did raise an interesting question. "This

might be a tad late to ask, but given we are compatible in the bedroom, does this mean you can get me pregnant?"

"Not currently. I have an implant to prevent my seed from taking root."

"What about disease?" Something she should have thought of earlier.

"The medical unit on my ship removes all traces of illness and contaminating microbes every time I return."

"So you're clean?"

"If I grasp your intent, then yes, but also getting impatient with all the questions."

Probably because he was still hard. "Poor, baby. Is someone horny?" she teased before flicking her tongue out to lick the tip of him.

While she'd known from the way he filled her pussy that he was built large, her up-close view really brought it home. His thick cock jutted from his hairless groin. As she lapped at his wide cap, she grasped him at the root. She felt him pulse in her grip, hard, so hard, and at her mercy.

The head, a darker color than the rest of him, barely fit into her mouth. She had to open extra wide, and he must have really enjoyed it because a strange flavor hit her tongue.

Sweet and salty. Yum.

Fingers fisted her hair as she drew him deeper, teasing him. How heady to hear this big, brash warrior groan as she played with his cock. It heightened her own pleasure to feel how tense his body grew the more she sucked him. And when she grazed her teeth along his length, he actually hissed.

"Don't stop," he murmured. "That feels good."

He sounded so surprised. Surely he'd gotten head before, or did aliens not indulge in oral foreplay?

It just made her more determined to pleasure him—and, in the process, she aroused herself.

Never had she taken such delight in giving her partner head. His taste, his texture, even his soft alien words of encouragement as he slipped into another tongue, only served to heighten her own building arousal.

Her mouth stretched—it had to as he grew larger—so impossibly wide. Oh how she longed to have him sink his massive dick into her pussy.

As if he read her mind, he manhandled her—or was it alien-handled? He yanked her to her feet and spun her until she faced the tile wall of the shower. The water, still warm, showered them, making their skin slippery. His foot spread her legs as far as they could in the tub. He palmed her lower belly, tilting her ass toward him. Her pussy throbbed in excitement as she felt the tip of his cock nudge at her nether lips.

"Stop teasing," she managed to gasp as he toyed with her, dipping his wide cap into her, only to just as quickly withdraw it.

"Impatient?"

"Horny. So get on with it."

A beep emitted from his wrist. Despite his

distracting dip in and out, she managed to focus enough to ask, "What's that sound for?"

"Possible company."

"What?"

"It seems someone has found us."

"We need to get dressed." She went to move, but his hands held her in place as he slid deeper.

"Not yet. I'm not done, and neither are you."

Was he serious? She craned to look at him and found him eyeing her with lids half-closed, his lips curved in the sexiest grin—one that should be outlawed because it made her agree to the most foolish thing.

Or act, she should say. Trusting he knew what he was doing—and, damn, was he doing it nice!—she tried not to think of someone barging in.

It should have doused her arousal like a bucket of cold water.

She should have snapped out of the moment.

Instead, she moaned as he sank deeper and deeper.

Yes, danger lurked. Yes, someone could barge in.

Oh god. It just excited her all the more.

She clawed at the slippery tile as he pounded into her willing flesh, each hard thrust butting her G-spot, making her channel clench, until with a yell, she came, her pussy milking his thickness.

She could have sworn she heard him growl

some kind of alien word before he jetted his hot cream, bathing her shuddering sex.

This time, there was no cuddling afterward. He dropped a kiss on her shoulder as he withdrew his cock. Then he slapped her on the ass and said, "You might want to hurry up and dress. They've just discovered we are not present in the first room and are now performing a room-by-room search."

Turning off the faucets first, she snagged a towel and hurriedly dried herself as she strode into their room. "What are we going to do? We can't exactly slip out unnoticed."

"Kill them."

"I thought you didn't have something to kill Mo and his mini-me."

"I don't yet, but those seeking us are just human."

She halted her drying to stare at him. "You mean the government guys found us?"

He nodded as he stepped into his jumpsuit—commando—and zipped.

She regarded her now grubby pants and shirt with a grimace, but her frown wasn't from trying to yank a T-shirt over damp boobs, but his solution. "Dude, you can't just kill them."

"Why not?"

"Well, because you can't. I mean they're just doing their job. Besides, won't killing them be like declaring some kind of alien war?"

His face turned pensive. "You might have a point. The galactic council would probably be most displeased if I annihilated Earth military forces.

They'd probably put out a universe-wide call for my execution or arrest."

"Exactly."

"How many do you think it would take for me to kill before achieving such a splendid feat?"

"Excuse me?" She gaped at him. "You can't seriously aspire to being a wanted criminal?"

"What warrior doesn't? Do you know what kind of glory I would bring to my family if I single-handedly had your planet declare war on my kind?"

"No."

"No what?"

"No, dude. No war. As in no killing. As in tuck your gun away. We'll have to sneak out of here."

"Are you seriously telling me what I may do?"

"Yup."

"A female giving me orders?" Incredulity marked his reply.

"Again yes. So stop giving me that face and think of a better plan, one that doesn't involve killing the men outside this door who are just doing their jobs."

"You are ruining what could be a momentous occasion and a highlight in my career."

"I'll blow you later in thanks."

"Why would you wish to eject air—" He stopped talking as she dropped her gaze to his groin. She licked her lips and then winked suggestively at him. "Oh, I think I understand your offer. Well, in that case..." He slid a tiny button on his weapon until it beeped and a blue light flashed.

"What did you just do?"

"Changed the setting from the laser setting to stun. I assume knocking them unconscious is acceptable?"

"Much better."

"The things I do for coitus," he muttered.

Disgruntled as he sounded, Jilly couldn't help a spurt of pleasure that he'd actually listened to her. Given his claims of how women were usually regarded, she considered it a positive feat he'd paid attention.

What she didn't consider so good, though, was the pounding on the door with the shouted, "Homeland Security. Open up."

Should they keep quiet and pretend the room was vacant?

A fine plan except for the fact that Vile—once again wearing his John Smith glamour—swung the door open and said, "Hello. It seems we meet again. If you value your lives, and physical wellbeing, then I strongly suggest you lay down your weapons."

# Chapter Eight

*"If someone calls you a pirate or a thief, kill them. Or, if you're feeling benevolent, or have cause to believe you might require their services in the future, correct them as to the correct terminology to use when referring to your professional title in the most painful method possible, of course. See Appendix Twelve for innovative ideas on torture." – An excerpt from The Fine Art of Acquisition*

Why did Jilly groan at his request? Vhyl worded his request to the humans at the door quite politely he thought. So politely his mother would have cried in shame. His father would have beaten him. As for the Earth agents facing him in the doorway? They laughed.

That wasn't a point in their favor.

"Nice try, bucko. We're the ones giving the orders here. Put down your tiny pistol and come out with your hands up."

"What is it with you humans and commenting on the size of my weapon?" Vhyl turned his gun over in his hand before tossing it on the bed and raising his hands.

"You too, Miss Carver," Agent Farley added. "Get the cuffs out, men. We're placing them under arrest."

"For what?" Jilly asked.

"I don't need a reason when we think

homeland security is at risk."

Sidling to his side, Jilly kept a wary eye on the pair of soldiers entering the room. "What are you doing surrendering?" she hissed as she placed her own hands in the air. "I thought your plan was to stun them so we could escape."

She seemed worried, whereas Vhyl didn't pay the soldiers much mind. As far as he was concerned, they should have sent more men. It was almost embarrassing how little his reputation counted here on Earth. Anywhere else in the galaxy, they would have sent three or four times the number. Now that would have been a much fairer fight. Then he might have also kept his weapon and told them where they could shove their order to surrender.

"Given I am unsure how the stun setting will work on your unenhanced genetic structure, I felt it best if I resort to simpler methods," he stated. He also felt it was more sporting. He allowed the two men to move behind him.

"Remember to not look him in the eye," barked Agent Farley, who wore dark-tinted glasses while the four men he'd brought with them all wore helmets with black visors.

Vhyl could not understand why Jilly began humming a melody that involved sunglasses at night under her breath. At his quizzical gaze, he thought she mouthed, 'Corey Hart'.

It made no sense, so he ignored it and focused on the men before him. Only the main agent didn't have a weapon in hand. Given Vhyl wore his repelling suit, he didn't worry much about the possibility of projectiles, unless one accidentally aimed for his head. Reconstructive surgery was never pleasant.

Jilly, on the other hand, didn't have any such protection, something he kept in mind as he planned his next move.

"Cuff the guy first," the one in charge ordered, still mistakenly thinking he controlled the situation.

It almost made Vhyl laugh. "You should have listened to me when you had the chance," he teased. That was the only warning they got before he punched one of the helmet-wearing soldiers in the face while, at the same time, kicking sideways, the boot of his suit connecting with another soldier's gun hand. The human cried out and dropped his weapon.

The one Vhyl punched still held his firearm, but his free hand attempted to stem the gush of blood from his nose.

Since he was occupied, Vhyl aimed a kick behind him at the male who thought to rush him from behind and slide an arm around his neck. A grab of the hand and a twist of his hips saw that soldier flying over Vhyl's shoulder to hit the floor with an oomph.

Just warming up, Vhyl aimed some rapid-fire thrusts and kicks at the remaining security force still standing, his movements too fast for them to counter. His mother had planned his genetic enhancements in the womb well. Perhaps he'd do something unprecedented when he returned and thank her for it. The shock alone would prove entertaining.

It took only a moment until the four soldiers were on the ground, three of them unconscious, the fourth moaning something about a broken hand.

Agent Farley gaped at him. "What the fuck are you?"

"Someone you need to forget," was Vhyl's reply before a well-aimed punch knocked the man unconscious.

Seeing no other immediate threat, Vhyl pivoted to find Jilly shaking her head. "Dude, you could make a fortune as an ultimate fighter."

"I already have great riches."

"Then why are you here looking for this hunk of metal?" she asked, holding up the disk.

"Because it's one of a kind."

"You mean you're going to all this trouble just to say you own it?"

"Of course. And then there's the excitement of guarding it well enough from those who would covet it. There is more to being an acquisition specialist than just ownership. Keeping what I've collected also requires great skill." It also made for some fun times as he toyed with thieves, faking easy access to some of his goods just so he could turn around and kill them for their temerity in trying.

A warrior created entertainment where he could. It helped keep his skills honed.

"You are whacked."

"I believe I shall take that as a compliment,"

Vhyl replied as he held out his hand in a courtly gesture. It was so utterly unlike him, and yet, he couldn't help warmth spreading at the smile Jilly gave him as he aided her in stepping around the prone bodies.

In the distance, sirens blared.

"You might want this," Jilly said, handing him his weapon. She'd also grabbed her own firearm, which he didn't understand given she seemed disinclined to shoot anyone.

As they clambered down the stairs, Vhyl noted the five agents weren't alone. Another trio hovered around the dark vehicles they'd arrived in.

At their appearance, the soldiers did not shout any foolish demand to surrender, but rather took aim and fired.

*About time they showed some common sense.*

And livened things up.

Vhyl had just enough time to thrust Jilly behind him before the first slug hit him in the chest—and bounced off his suit.

Still though. They'd dared to shoot at him!

Forget running away. For their temerity, he'd make them pay. It elated him to note the day was looking up.

Tucking his gun away—since hitting things with his bare hands was so much more fun—Vhyl dashed at the soldiers, who fired again. It only served to stir him up. Vhyl yelled an ancient Aressotle war cry, which, if translated, amounted to, "I'm going to kill you and drink of your blood then hunt down your family and annihilate your line." Of course, he probably wouldn't have time to do the latter, and given Jilly's reminder about starting a war, he stuck to knocking the soldiers unconscious.

*I really should get a second war cry for the times when I'm only causing chaos and not murdering those who stand in my way.*

Something to ponder during the boring moments in between acquisitions.

Jilly joined him. "Dude, you are a fighting machine."

Did he puff his chest at the compliment? Yes. And he also dragged her into his arms for a kiss that left her breathless.

He only released her as the wailing vehicle screeched into the far end of the parking lot.

"We should leave," he stated unnecessarily.

"Says the guy who stopped to steal a kiss," she muttered as she jumped into the driver's seat of her truck. "You really like living on the edge, don't you?"

"Any other way is not worth living." He grinned as she shook her head.

Despite her admonishment, he caught the hint of a smile on her lips. Even more fascinating, her pulse raced, but he'd have wagered it was in excitement not fear.

His female barbarian thrived more on adventure than she let on.

She also drove like one of those insane Veloxrians who seemed to think traffic rules were meant to be broken.

"Now who is the crazy one?" he shouted as

she weaved among the cars on the two-lane route they were on.

"Still you. But I'm beginning to think it's contagious," she added with a laugh. "You know, given you just took out some government dudes and I am now fleeing the cops, I should be freaking out."

"But?" he prodded.

"I don't think I've ever had so much fun," she admitted.

"You were made for this kind of lifestyle."

"Maybe in your world. In mine, this kind of lifestyle would either kill me or see me landing in jail."

"You could come with me when I leave." He made the offer spuriously and, for a moment, wondered if he'd had his body taken over by some kind of spirit. But no. As far as he could ascertain, he was in control of his mental faculties. *Which means I meant it.*

When he dissected the idea further, he could see how Jilly would prove a fascinating companion to bring along on his travels.

There was just one problem with his plan. She didn't want to come.

"Sorry, dude, but no thanks. I might drive like a speed demon, but even I know that leaving my planet and everything I know to fly off into space with an almost virtual stranger is nuts. I mean, we barely know each other."

"I would beg to differ. I can state with assurance that I am familiar with most aspects of your body."

"That's physical. I'll admit, when it comes to sex, we are extremely compatible. But a relationship needs more than that to work. I'm talking about the other stuff, the mental shit. Like love and friendship."

"What does that have to do with joining me?"

"Everything. The very fact you don't grasp it is why I can't go. Maybe aliens like you don't get the whole love thing, but with humans, it's huge. Really huge," she added as she swerved around a large truck, only to confront an even bigger one coming at them head-on.

For a moment as she spun the steering contraption, the vehicle lifted and teetered on two wheels before slamming back down.

How Vhyl missed the more stable method of travel exhibited by hovercrafts.

"Are you claiming you love me?" And why did the thought elate him?

"Of course not. It's too soon for that. But, in order for me to give up my life here, my home, everything I know, I should at least hope the possibility of love between us exists."

He couldn't help but make a face. "Affection makes a warrior weak."

"I highly doubt that. And even if that were the case, it's different for humans. We need affection to thrive."

"I cannot promise you that."

"Then I guess we're at an impasse."

"So you are saying no, even though we would have grand adventures together?"

For a moment she didn't reply, and when she did, she let out a big sigh first. "Yeah, it's a no."

While the scream of sirens had faded as Jilly's expert maneuvering with her archaic land transport gained them a lead, Vhyl could still spot the red and blue flashes of her police force following in the distance.

"We should turn off this road when an alternate route becomes available and see if we can lose our pursuers."

"Good plan."

With no warning, she spun the wheel, sending the back end of the truck fishtailing before its tires caught the pavement and they shot off in another direction, one lined with trees and dark.

Vhyl held on to the dash, certain he was about to die.

But Jilly managed to keep them upright and on the road.

A miracle.

His wristband beeped.

"What now?" she asked. "More enemies coming?"

"No. My vessel has made it into your airspace and is currently tracking me overhead. If we can find a large open area, it will only take a few moments of stoppage for it to lower enough to transport me aboard."

"Leaving already?" She sounded so disappointed. Before he could reply, she snorted.

"Of course you're leaving. There's nothing keeping you here. You found the artifact. And it's probably best you go before you start some kind of alien war."

True, yet he found himself reluctant to go. Things felt unfinished between him and his barbarian. "There is the question of payment."

She waved a hand at him. "Forget it. I'll consider the fact I'm alive and that you gave me the adventure of a lifetime payment enough. Beside, the quicker you're gone, the quicker I can go back to my old life."

Odd. She refused to leave with him and live a life of adventure and yet, at the same time, seemed less than enthused at the prospect of staying.

And he thought the females of his planet were complicated.

It seemed they'd lost their pursuers for the moment. No lights gleamed behind them, and they only passed the occasional pair heading in the opposite direction.

When the forest opened up, the moon chose that moment to unveil itself, illuminating the world in a white glow that reflected off the snow on the ground. A poetic male would have found the scenery beautiful and probably waxed eloquent—which meant Vhyl would have had to kill him. He did so hate the artsy types.

Jilly pulled to the side of the road and did something to extinguish the lights shining from the front of her truck, but she left the engine running, probably so they wouldn't run out of heat. Her world was cold.

However, the low temperature wasn't why she shivered. She might claim they were still almost strangers, but Vhyl begged to differ.

In their short time together, he'd learned to read his human. To understand the varied emotions she expressed, both with her face and body language.

Vhyl slid his hand around her nape and drew her close to him, wondering if he could change her mind with a kiss, as he found himself reluctant to leave her.

It made no sense.

*I want her.*

Not because she would complement his collection of rare and priceless things.

Not because, as an attractive human, she'd fetch a high price on the Obsidian market.

Not because she was a fabulous coital partner—although it did help.

Vhyl wanted her because, despite their short acquaintance, he felt a connection to Jilly. An urge to discover the different facets of her personality. A desire to further explore her intriguing personality and nature. A need to protect her imbued him. A jealousy that another might kiss those lips burned him.

So many things he felt.

*Felt?*

What the frukx?

Was he suffering from the human emotion she kept calling love?

*Argh. I've caught an Earthling disease.*

Yet oddly enough he didn't crave a cure.

He thought all these things as he kissed her, but he said nothing aloud. Warriors did not speak of their mental turmoil. They did not admit to emotion unless it was to tell their enemy how much they hated them and looked forward to disemboweling them.

A warrior most certainly never told a female that a lifetime without her seemed bleak and not worth living.

The air in the truck steamed with the frenzy of their kiss. Just about to yank her onto his lap to see if they could contort themselves enough to indulge in carnal play, he could have shot down his own vessel when it suddenly arrived, hovering overhead and drenching the outside in darkness as it blocked the glow from the moon.

Jilly pulled away from the kiss first. In a soft voice she said, "Your ride is here."

"Come with me." He didn't quite beg, but he winced at his request, unable to believe he'd asked yet again.

His weakness when it came to this female was revolting, and yet he couldn't help it. He wanted her.

She didn't immediately say no. "What if I did and things didn't work out?"

"Then I would return you. My word." Which, despite his mercenary ways, was worth its weight in precious gems.

Warriors rarely made a promise, but when

they did, honor made them keep it. Some thought that odd, given their penchant for rule breaking, but as the mercenary handbook said in one of its many education chapters, "Breaking a vow is easy. Too easy. A true mercenary takes the harder path always."

"I don't know. Maybe we—"

Whatever reply she meant to give was lost as an explosion rocked the ground. Her truck trembled.

"What the fuck was that?" she yelled.

After all they'd been through, she really had to ask?

"My enemy, of course."

# Chapter Nine

*"Don't be stupid. If someone is shooting at you, take cover." – Grandpa's not often heard philosophy because Grandma usually slapped him in the arm and said, "Shut up, Merle. Everyone knows the smart thing to do is fire on the bastards and take 'em out."*

When Vile dove out of the truck, Jilly didn't immediately follow. One, because she was still stunned by his request she go with him, and two, there was a fucking alien shooting laser beams, which really didn't seem conducive to staying alive.

Wouldn't you know, one of them sliced across the hood of her truck. More than sliced, it carved off the whole front end, which hit the ground with a thump.

*My truck. My precious baby.*

Killed. By a fucking jelly-tentacled Martian.

If ever she'd wished for a flamethrower—and had Grandma lived she'd have surely wrapped one for Jilly under the Christmas tree—it was now.

Vile ripped open the driver door. "Are you trying to die? Get out of the frukxing vehicle."

Since her truck seemed a target rather than a haven, Jilly obeyed. Two feet on the shaking ground, though, didn't mean she knew where to go. Exactly where did Vile think she could flee that was safe? An open field, with singed furrows in the snow, didn't exactly provide cover.

He noted her hesitation and deduced the cause. "Head for my ship," he yelled. "I will hold Mo and his progeny off."

Easier said than done considering his enemy was making snow melt with wild sweeps of his laser gun.

When one made the toe of her boot smoke because the glowing ray came so close, she retreated back to the shadow of her truck, where at least she didn't make such an inviting target. It also blocked her view of what was happening, though. Standing behind a wheel, lest she lose more than a toe if a laser swept beneath the undercarriage, she peeked over the truck bed.

One big purple dude in a space jumpsuit racing full-tilt across the road, yelling some battle cry? Check.

One human gaping in astonishment and wondering how she'd gone from worrying about the bank foreclosing to staying alive in an alien attack? Check-ing into a mental asylum because she was sure no one would ever believe her.

How Vile managed to dodge the laser burst, she couldn't have said. Each time she blinked against the brightness, he was in a different spot while his last location smoked a crater.

Given his hands were empty, she wondered what he planned. Somehow she didn't think choking Jelly dude would prove effective.

But Vile had a different plan in mind.

He aimed his finger at Mo, and in the

sudden silence that came between the laser bursts, she could have sworn she heard him say. "Bang. You're dead."

Less bang and more like sizzle. But not from Vile's purple digit.

His spacecraft was the one to shoot a molten stream of fire. At least she assumed the blue and white streak was fire, given it hit Mo and ignited the tentacled blob. With only a tiny squeal—kind of anticlimactic if you asked her—jelly guy melted into a bubbling glob of goo. Glowing green goo, which she'd bet was radioactive, and would probably cause some interesting crops to grow in that spot next spring.

(Actually, as it turned out, according to the news she read a year later, the area had the oddest infestation of waggling, almost tentacle eared bunnies who seemed to be multiplying quicker than usual.)

Given the fate of his sire, Mini-me tried to run. Or slither. Whatever you called his attempt to escape, it failed and he suffered the same fate. Poor thing.

Not.

A quiet swept the land, even though a giant saucer hovered overhead. Neat technology those engines of Vhyl that didn't even rumble. But not as cool as the purple hunk striding toward her.

A hunk who frowned in displeasure.

"I thought I told you to get on my ship."

"One. I would have died before making it. Two. Exactly how do you get on the damned thing?" Because she didn't see a ramp or stairs. Hell, it didn't even have a cool tractor beam thing like most sci-fi movies portrayed.

"I forget you know little of our technology."

"Try knows nothing of your technology." And never would. The reminder kind of depressed her. She scuffed a foot across the ground. "So I guess this is goodbye."

"You won't come with me?"

Here he was asking again. Did she dare take a chance and—

Sirens wailed in the distance. Time grew short. She needed to make a decision, so she brashly asked, "Do you think you'll ever love me?"

The answer, while expected, still hurt. "Of course not. Love is a human emotion. But I do want you."

Disappointment slumped her shoulders. "Want isn't enough. Just because you want something doesn't mean you should have it." Or that she should leave everything she'd ever known.

What about when he no longer felt the burning need? What would happen to her when he awoke one day and moved on to pinker pastures— or, in his case, maybe purple ones?

"Are you denying me?"

"I'm not coming with you."

"Just because I won't admit to a human frailty?" The concept seemed to flabbergast him.

"No, because I deserve more out of life than to be something a man wants to own. I deserve to be loved."

"I would take care of you. Pleasure you. Shower you with presents."

"It's not enough. Not for me. Go, Vile. Go back to your world." One she didn't belong in.

He frowned. He really was pulling out all his adorable stops, but she fought his allure.

"You're being obstinate, Jilly."

"No, I'm being human."

Red lights and blue lights strobed in the distance, but they were less ominous than the stuttering sound of a helicopter, make that more than one. The military was closing in.

"You should leave before they catch you," she said.

"As if they could," he scoffed.

No, but they could destroy his vessel.

With no heed for the danger—damn him for being so sexy—he drew her to his chest and kissed her.

The heat of it almost changed her mind. It definitely weakened her knees.

Then lights were upon them as cars screeched to a halt and doors slammed.

Vile released her, his eyes glowing. He opened his mouth and shut it. His lips thinned. "Goodbye, Jilly."

He turned and began to sprint, only to abruptly stop when she yelled, "Aren't you forgetting something?"

He whirled, his face inquiring, his reflexes perfect as she tossed the artifact to him. He caught it, but strangely, he seemed almost disappointed.

They stared at each other.

Stared long enough for men to rush and line the field, yelling about surrendering.

With a gesture of his hand at the soldiers and cops that was probably the human equivalent of 'fuck you', Vile leapt into the air, an incomprehensible act until the beam of light shot from the belly of his ship and engulfed him.

Blinded, Jilly shut her eyes against the brilliance, and when she opened them again…

He was gone.

*He left.*

And it made her chest ache something fierce.

Despite their short whirlwind of an acquaintance, she'd grown fond of him and would miss him. Especially now with cops flooding the place and sure to bombard her with questions—right after they arrested her.

She didn't bother to run. Run where? Her house blew up. And how? Her car sat in two pieces, scrap metal at best.

Even more depressed, she sat on the tailgate of her truck, only to find herself ignored.

While lights swept over her, and a swarm of people tramped in the next field over where Mo's remains glowed disturbingly, no one spoke to her, or even acknowledged her.

*It's as if I'm invisible.*

A theory she tested in the chaos that followed Vhyl's departure.

Somehow, Jilly managed to avoid getting

arrested. It could have been because, while one space saucer disappeared, another was discovered across the road in the other field. Mo's neon grave also drew lots of attention. Or maybe her lucky spell had to do with the wristband Vile had slipped on her during their kiss.

Whatever the reason, it was almost as if she wore some kind of invisibility glamor, one that allowed her to walk away from the area unchallenged.

Alone, and downcast, the adrenaline wearing off, she wandered away from the scene of chaos.

Eventually, her spell of invisibility, or whatever it was that let her escape unseen, wore off because she managed to hitch a ride, several as a matter of fact, which, given her ragged state, was a bit of a surprise. Or not, given at least one guy needed a black eye to learn "Don't touch" meant don't fucking touch.

Almost twelve hours later, her last ride dropped her off at her farm. Her poor destroyed farm.

In between the explosion of the farmhouse, the vehicles that had run amok, first putting out the fire then investigating, the entire area was a churned-up mess of snow, mud, and debris.

*And to think I turned Vile down to come back to this.*

At least with him, she would have enjoyed some pleasure, at least for a while. But in the end, she preferred to nurse her broken heart here among her own kind than later when she was well and truly lost—and she didn't mean just in space.

She couldn't have said how long she stared at the ruined mess.

A vehicle drove up behind her, and still she didn't move. Where would she go? She'd thrown away her chance at a new life.

*Stupidest move ever.*

"Miss Jillian Carver?"

*Oh you've got to be fucking kidding me.*

Could her day get any worse?

Perhaps if she ignored him, he'd go away.

Nope.

"Miss Carver, I know you can hear me."

Unfortunately. She pivoted to behold the prick she'd been dealing with at the bank. Less dealing and more like begging for more time. Time that he denied.

Flanked by a pair of cops, he held a sheaf of papers in his hand.

"What do you want?" she asked, unable to hide her irritation.

"Since you failed to pay the sum owing on your mortgage, it is my sad duty to inform you this property is now the possession of the bank."

"You're foreclosing? But I thought I still had a few days."

"It is our right, especially given the willful damage done to the property in the past few days, to change the date. It's right here in the contract."

He pointed to a small blob of text, which she was sure in some legal mumbo-jumbo backed his words.

"But it's Christmas Eve." A fact she'd almost forgotten in the turmoil but suddenly remembered as a glint of melted gold winked from the rubble.

"We wanted to get this settled before the end of the business day. As of this moment, you no longer own this land."

A few days ago she might have ranted and raved. Maybe even resorted to tears.

But now?

She didn't care.

On the contrary, knowing the farm, and all its problems, was being taken from her actually lightened the load. She was free. Free from the crushing debt of it. Free from its maintenance and headaches and everything that came with owning land she couldn't care for. Land that kept her from being free.

Would her grandmother turn over in her grave?

Probably. But then again, Grandma freaked when alive over lots of things.

She also knew her grandmother would have never wanted Jilly to suffer or feel trapped.

Of course, now that Jilly was homeless, and had her epiphany moment where she realized she could go anywhere and do anything, she really wished she'd gone with Vile.

So what if their relationship lasted, one day, one month, or forever? So what if he thought he couldn't love? Perhaps she could have taught him.

*I could have seen and done things no one ever*

*imagined.*

What an adventure. What a man. What a fucking loss.

Sigh.

As the bank prick departed with his armed escort, but not before administering an admonishment to clear the property by midnight, she found herself well and truly alone.

In the cold.

No money.

Sans wheels.

Without a thing to her name.

So was it any wonder when the beam of light shot down from the sky, she smiled.

*He came back for me.*

Just one problem.

It wasn't the right he.

# Chapter Ten

*What's mine is mine. What's yours is mine. What's his is mine. And if it's not mine, it's not worth having. - Vhyl's personal philosophy on life.*

"Mentally stunted, perversely stubborn, frukxing female," Vhyl couldn't help but curse as he boarded his ship without Jilly.

He cursed, but not because the human forces had spotted him and his ship.

He cursed, but not because Jilly handed him the XiiX without payment or a fight, which made its acquisition kind of unexciting.

He cursed because he'd left her.

Alone.

*Because she didn't want to come.*

Since when did that frukxing matter?

A true warrior took what he wanted. He didn't listen to the pleading or screaming. He didn't care about another being's thoughts or feelings on the mater.

Look at his distant cousins. Tren, Jaro, the idiot duo, his competitive partner, Makl, even that lackwit who wanted to be a hero, Dyre. Most of them had abducted their brides. Each of them saw a female, a human one like Jilly, who would give them what they needed, and they took action. They abducted their woman and didn't accept no for an answer.

Vhyl, on the other hand, respected her wishes. Probably because some Earth parasite was chewing at what wits he had left.

Stupid alien planet.

But if it were some kind of disease or bug, then that meant there was a cure. He rushed himself into the decontamination chamber, hoping the various cleansing options would remove the turmoil going through his mind.

While he emerged sanitized and clean, he couldn't purge himself of the illogic that led to him leaving her behind.

Nor did it make his need of the barbarian human lessen.

Subjecting himself to the invasive probing of a medical unit, searching for some deeper reason for his mental incapacity, also came up negative.

*I still want her.*

And by all the planets he'd seeded disharmony on, he would have her.

Frukx her wishes on the matter. Vhyl was the Black Hole of Aressotle. What he coveted, he took. Take her he would, and he knew just where to find her.

With the wrist communication device he'd given her during their last moment together to afford her some measure of protection against her own people, he could track her movements. It would allow him to swoop back at his leisure and abduct her. Not give her a choice.

*You will be mine.*

Just not right yet. First, he needed to take

care of a minor problem. Namely Mo's ship.

During his quest to regain his cutthroat side via medical and scientific means, the humans had surrounded the dead alien's vessel with a miniature army. Large trucks arrived spilling soldiers. Bright lights were set up and cast a glare on the landed craft. Men in uniforms barked orders while others ran around to no purpose Vhyl could ascertain.

The excitement over their discovery was palpable but would be short-lived.

Despite Vhyl's pleasure when it came to rule breaking, even he didn't dare violate the prime directive. *Do not let barbarians get their hands on our technology.* Mo's vessel, even if archaic in design, could not remain in their possession. Humans weren't ready for that kind of knowledge yet.

So, Vhyl did the only thing he could. Directing a concentrated beam of energy at the grounded ship, he melted it.

While this method wouldn't have worked on his vessel or anything built in recent times, Mo's ship was a much older design, which meant it wasn't constructed with the toughest materials. Under the concerted heat of his laser, it slowly collapsed— despite the screams of the humans running around in a panic—into a slag of junk.

While he performed this task, slowly because he didn't want to accidentally kill any humans—talk about ruining his fun—various aerial crafts tried to penetrate the protective shield around his ship. Their puny weapons system could do nothing.

The one thing Vhyl could not prevent was

the various videos that captured his ship's presence, but, given it had no identifying markers, the council would have a hard time pinning the crime on him.

*Perhaps I should send them a memo so they know who to attribute the breach of their rules to.*

Tren, a distant Aressotle cousin who sat on the council—and led it after killing those who dared to stand in his way—would probably place a bounty on his head.

Or, as the warriors on his planet called it, crown him with great honor and a promise of fun times.

The procedure to destroy Mo's ship took many Earth hours, more than he liked. It meant Jilly had plenty of time to relocate—and get into trouble.

How he liked that facet of her personality.

Setting his sensors to track the signal on the wristband he gave her—which she hopefully hadn't ditched—he went in search of his female. And when he found her, he'd take her, even if she protested. He almost hoped she did.

If she wanted to fight his choice, then it would make the coitus they'd indulge in later all the sweeter as he showed her the positive aspect to her abduction.

He ran into a problem though with his plan.

Someone got to her first.

Someone dared to take his human.

*SOMEONE. TOOK. MY. FEMALE.*

In other words, someone had declared war on Vhyl and was about to die.

# Chapter Eleven

*"Who cares if it's Christmas morning, Jilly-bean. Those cows ain't going to milk themselves." – Grandma, who always acted tough, yet always left a present in the stall with Bitsy their cow.*

As Christmas mornings went, Jilly was probably having the worst one ever.

*And I thought the year Grandma gave me a Barbie instead of the crossbow I asked for sucked.*

Abducted by a space pirate, which she might add looked like a cross between a crocodile and a man, with stubby arms and an actual tail, who seemed to think he could use her as leverage to get Vile to trade the artifact—not likely given his mercenary code of ethics—or, if that didn't work, sell her as a rare delicacy to some race who craved human flesh, Jilly was really regretting her wish on that false star.

Yeah, her life had changed. Yeah, she didn't have to worry about the farm anymore. But she couldn't say her situation had improved.

*My own fault for turning down my purple hunk.*

How she wished she could go back in time and replay that decision. However, there was no use crying over spilt milk. *Get out there and milk the damned cow again,* her grandmother would say. Except, in this case, she didn't have a cow to squeeze, and she certainly wasn't about to cozy up to her captor.

Seven-foot, talking crocs, with plain evil yellow eyes, just weren't attractive.

And her second impression of Snaggle Tooth, her name for him since she couldn't pronounce the gibberish he'd introduced himself with, didn't improve. Ordered from her cell by a gang of pigs, or at least descendants of pigs with their snout noses, black beady eyes, and tusks growing from their mouths, Jilly wondered at her fate.

*Will they keep me alive until they deliver me to those aliens who want to eat me as dessert?*

*Freeze dry me to keep me fresh?*

*Fatten me up to charge more per pound?*

Nothing wrong with her imagination.

Yet she would have never imagined what she'd see when she entered the command center of the ship. While replete with fascinating *Star Trek*-type displays and equipment—lots of flashing lights, dials and buttons, all begging for her to push them—what really caught her attention was the huge view screen on the wall. A live video feed of none other than Vile.

Sigh. How she missed his handsome, purple presence. How she hated him for putting her in this predicament. How she wished, once more, she'd not been such a freaking idiot.

His placid expression only twitched for a millisecond when he spotted her.

Was he happy to see her? Mad? Worried?

She couldn't tell. Nor did she dare guess. As far as she was concerned, he wasn't there out of any concern for her. He was only making an appearance because Snaggle Tooth had called him.

*He doesn't know how to love. He said so himself.* But did that mean he didn't care?

Despite his nonchalant demeanor, she noted Vile's fingers drumming the armrest to his chair. Unlike what she'd expected, his seat resembled more of a La-Z-Boy recliner than any kind of captain's chair in a spaceship.

Snaggle Tooth grabbed her by the shoulder and pulled her until she stood right in front of the large screen. "As requested, here is my proof I am in possession of the human female."

"So I see. And?"

"And, if you do not give me the artifact, I will kill her." Snaggle Tooth said it with way too much relish.

"You do know who I am?" Vile asked, again seeming so calm, but was it just Jilly, or did his eyes harbor a hint of rage?

"I know of you."

A sigh and a roll of Vile's eyes made his next words almost comical. "Then you should already know how this conversation goes. You make demands I trade the treasure for the girl. I remind you that she is simply an expendable female. You try to convince me of her worth on the Obsidian market. I nonchalantly reply that I am rich beyond belief and don't care. Whereupon, you make threats, I get annoyed, and blow your ship to small pieces."

A sly expression entered Snaggle Tooth's mien, which meant he went from pretty ugly to really ugly. "The old Black Hole who built a reputation on thievery and killing might have blown my ship up, along with all its occupants. However, I am going to wager the new one won't."

"Then you will lose that bet, and your life. I hope your estate is in order, as you are going to die today."

The certainty with which he said it sent a shiver down Jilly's spine.

"I think you're bluffing. I know for a fact you were tracking the girl's movements. It's why I took her, and it's why you followed me out of the Earth's star system."

*Hold on, did crocodile dude just say Vile was stalking me?*

Hope fluttered in her breast.

Vile scowled. "And to think those bastards on Lojica claimed no one could detect me on radar."

"No one except someone with a Lojica radar system," said Snaggle Tooth with a wide smile consisting of too many sharp teeth.

"I see I shall have to upgrade my detection system, or eradicate everyone else's. As to your claim I was tracking the female? I was merely ensuring her well-being so as to prevent an intergalactic war from breaking out."

Now it was Jilly's turn to frown. Was it her or did his reply make no sense?

It seemed she wasn't the only one to find fault with his reason.

"Enough of the lies. You want the girl. I have her. Either you give me the artifact, or she dies."

Enough of the dick waving. Time for her to step in and see if she couldn't salvage a way to stay alive.

"Um, excuse me, but don't I get a say in this?"

The dual-snapped "No!" didn't shut her up, although, it did incite her temper.

"Fuck you both," she snapped. "I will not have the pair of you discussing my future as if my wants in the matter don't count. Is it too much to ask that I get a say in this? It is, after all, Christmas fucking day. A day that is supposed to be about giving, and the only thing you're both giving me is a goddamned headache."

"Silence, girl," Snaggle Tooth boomed, but she didn't cower.

Fear wouldn't free her. Neither would stubbornness. But Grandma didn't raise her to sit quietly by as others decided her fate.

"Oh don't you tell me to shut up, Mr. Would-Look-So-Much-Better-As-A-Handbag. You," she stabbed a finger at lizard man, "are the reason why we're having this discussion. You had no right to kidnap me or to threaten me or offer me as a canapé for some alien buffet. I have rights. Or so some galactic council with all kinds of laws claims. I know for a fact I am a protected species. I demand you return me to my home before I report you." Which she wasn't sure how she'd accomplish, but it was the best threat she could think of given she didn't have access to a gun. How she missed

Problem Solver.

She caught Vile's on-screen snicker, and she turned her glare on him next.

"Don't be so quick to laugh there, mister. After all we shared, I can't believe you'd let me die so you could keep some stupid artifact. To think I was actually regretting not choosing to go with you. And even stupider me for believing, for a second when I saw you on-screen, that you cared enough to come save me."

"You want to be with me?"

"Yeah. Or I did. Now I just want to slap you."

"Kind of hard to accomplish, given you're over there and I'm over here," he pointed out.

"No duh."

"Don't give me attitude, woman. It was your choice to stay behind, and I allowed it out of," he made a face, "respect for your wishes, even if it went against all my planet's teachings. If I'd behaved like a proper mercenary, I would have abducted you."

"Why didn't you? I'll tell you why. It's obviously because you don't care about me. If you did, you would have ignored my protests, swept me off my feet, and carried me off. Or is that flew me away? Whatever, it doesn't matter. Fact is you left without really any fight. Some warrior you are."

"Take that back. I am the fiercest warrior you will ever know."

"Says the guy who didn't even try to force me to go with him."

"A mistake. One I intended to fix. I'll have you know I came back."

"Too late, which means your change of heart does me little good now."

"Do you truly wish you'd come with me?" He asked her so seriously.

For a moment she thought of telling him no. But, given she was about to die, what could it hurt to give him the truth? "Yeah, I wish I'd said yes. But like Grandma always said, wishes don't grow on trees. Apples do, and if I don't stop mooning about what I can't have, she'll throw a bushel of them at me."

Not exactly the warmest sentiment, but it made Vile grin. "I think I would have liked your grandmother."

Oddly enough, Jilly would have wagered Grandma would have liked him, too.

"Since we both made mistakes, let us start over. What will it take to convince you that I truly do care about you?"

"What do you think?" She glanced around her, sticking her tongue out at Snaggle Tooth, who seemed utterly stymied by their verbal byplay.

"Very well, my barbarian. Fazird, despite the stain on my reputation, and the tears my mother will cry at my capitulation, I agree to surrender the XiiX to you in exchange for the human. Unharmed."

"You do?"

He did?

They all seemed surprised. Even Vile. "It is to the shame of my family that I admit a certain affection for the barbarian. Probably a disease I picked up during my time planet-side, one I can't seem to rid myself of. Nonetheless, my need for her is potent. Possibly terminal and most definitely emasculating. I shall require many deaths to make up for this weakness lest it tarnish my reputation."

Not exactly the most romantic declaration, but it was a start.

Things moved quickly after that. In no time at all, she was standing in some kind of pressurized airlock, Snaggle Tooth holding her upper arm in a tight grip, which had her on tiptoe, given his short arms but extreme height.

His piggy crew—which weren't as adorable as the Muppets' Pigs in Space version—had their guns aimed, half on her, half on the door.

*Click. Hiss. Whirr.*

The silence was broken only by the machine sounds as a docking tube was sent from Vile's ship to Snaggle's, or so they explained when she asked how they planned to make the trade, given she wasn't exactly sure they had a spacesuit in her size.

The door slid open, and there was Vile. More handsome than ever, wearing an open-necked white shirt, tight-fitting black breeches, and dark boots that went almost to his knees.

He appeared rakish and completely at ease. The jerk. And here she was dirty and still wearing the same rags.

He held up the coveted disk, which glinted benignly. All this trouble over a stupid ornament that had hung on her Christmas tree for years.

The grip around her upper arm tightened. "How do I know it's the real thing?" Snaggle asked.

Vile rolled his eyes. "Oh please. Don't tell me your detection unit hasn't already scanned it for authenticity." His expression hardened. "Now release my woman."

*My woman.* How she liked the sound of that.

With a flick of his wrist, Vile sent the artifact spinning in the air.

Thrust from Snaggle Tooth, Jilly stumbled...right into her purple dude's arms. He hugged her to him, and she hugged him back.

"The treasure is mine," crowed her lizard captor. "Disengage the ships."

"Double crossing bastard." Vile only barely managed to get them in the passageway before the door slid shut.

"Why that two timing, jerk!" she huffed.

"Hate him later. Now we must run before we are sucked into space."

*Excuse me?*

No time for questions. Vile tossed her over his shoulder and ran along the connecting tube while air hissed behind them.

"What's happening?" she squeaked.

"He's pressurizing the lock. Once it's done, he's going to release our passageway."

"That sounds bad."

"Only if you're a flesh-based organism."

"Then run faster," she yelled.

"Bossy female," he grumbled. Yet he did put on even more speed. Just enough, too, because he'd no sooner slid them into another airlock and slapped a button to shut the door than a cold breeze whipped up behind them and then whistled as it tried to suck them back out.

Luckily the door sealed the portal shut before they could become Popsicles in space.

Leaving her with her purple alien.

"Now what?" she asked, as he didn't seem inclined to put her back down.

"Now we hit the decontamination chamber, barbarian. You reek."

# Chapter Twelve

*"Every collector has a prized possession, the one item he would protect with his life and keep above all others. When you find it, guard it fiercely, cherish it, and enjoy it. It's yours. Your treasure."*
*An excerpt from The Fine Art of Acquisition.*

Perhaps he should have not referred to her less than odorous condition. As he deposited Jilly in the decontamination chamber, she glared at him.

"You really don't know how to sweet talk a girl."

"Why would I speak sweetly? I am a male, not a woman or a politician."

"Oh, you're a man all right. One with a one-track mind," she added as he literally tore the clothes from her body exposing her, and he also tweaked her nipples in the process. Who could resist the pert buds?

He quickly shed his own garments, displaying his erection.

"I have missed you." Surprise, he didn't choke making the admission.

"I missed you, too, but I'll admit I'm kind of baffled by the fact you're going to waste time in here with me when Snaggle Tooth is getting away with your prize."

"Are you so sure of that?"

"I feel like I'm missing something."

"No. We are just in time."

Vhyl placed his hand on a depression in the wall, and the opaque white surface turned into a video screen, one showing space, and a certain alien vessel.

"Is that—"

"Fazird's ship, yes."

"Is he firing on us?" Jilly asked.

"Yes." He noted her puzzled expression. "I have the shields engaged. None of his puny weaponry can penetrate it. Now watch."

The explosion was sudden. The enemy ship on screen exploded, the intensity of it enough to send a tremble through his own vessel.

She laughed. "Take that, sucker! I'm going to take a guess here and say you blew him up?"

"Of course. As if I'd let him live after allowing him to see my ignoble and first ever defeat at the hands of a female."

"You mean you killed him because he heard you admit you cared for me."

"Yes."

She snickered. "Dude, that is seriously warped."

"I also couldn't allow him to live because he dared touch you."

"Not into sharing?"

"I don't share what is mine."

"It's funny you should say that," she said with a smile. "Because I've got jealousy issues too, and I'm telling you right now that while we're together you better forget all those other alien bitches."

"Only the canine-based ones?" he asked with a frown.

"All females."

"Your jealousy is quite becoming." And it was. The malicious glint in her eyes, the evil twisted smile as she implied murderous intent.

He could not resist a moment longer. As the cleansing waves of the decontamination unit swept them, he yanked her into his arms and bent his head to embrace her, hungry for a taste of her. She met him with a fierce passion, leaning up on her toes so as to fully engage him in the kiss.

In but moments, both their breaths emerged in fast pants, her power to arouse him as stupendous as always. He sucked at her full lower lip while her hands clung at this neck, drawing him closer.

Slipping his tongue past the seam of her lips, he passed it over her blunt-edged teeth before engaging hers. The moist twining of their flesh only served to fuel his need for more. More of her.

Urgency made him greedy to skip some of the pleasures in foreplay so he could claim her, this time in a more permanent fashion than ever before. His hands clasped her waist, and he lifted her so that he could position her against the wall. With Jilly pinned there, he moved his grip to her buttocks, cupping their full roundness and kneading.

The softness of her skin never failed to delight him, but her eager cries of pleasure enraptured him. She devoured his mouth and sucked on his tongue with passion. It awed him still that her level of desire seemed to match his own. Ever better it was neither feigned nor contrived. It wasn't paid for. *She wants me.*

With her braced against the wall, he could easily support her with one arm anchored around her waist. Good thing because he needed one free so he could check the level of arousal in her sex.

Moist.

Hot.

Quivering.

He could have shuddered with the evidence of her readiness for him.

As per their previous encounter, toying with the nub at the mouth of her sex caused her to mewl and squirm.

"Vile." She groaned his name, still pronouncing it with her Earth accent, but he'd gotten used to it. Liked it even. Not as much as her reaction to his continued tease of her nub.

Despite her squirming plea, he didn't slide himself in. Not yet. Not when he so enjoyed feeling her pleasure as he stroked her faster and faster. How he loved hearing her cries come quicker, more frantic.

Thrusting a finger into her sex caused a shudder to sweep her, one he felt around his penetrating digit.

Tight. So tight. And ready for him. Ready for him to sheath his cock and pound.

He could hold off no longer. He guided his cock to rub against the mouth of her sex, wetting the swollen tip.

"Stop teasing and fuck me," she demanded, an order he didn't bristle at given she said it with swollen lips and eyes languorous with desire.

He held off, needing to hear something from her. "Say you are mine."

"I'm yours."

"All mine."

"All yours," she said vehemently as she grabbed at his head and drew him in for a violent kiss.

It proved his undoing. He slammed into her, his throbbing cock entering her willing channel in one smooth stroke, which had her clawing at him and crying out.

For a moment, he thought she'd come, but while she tensed and her breathing was ragged, she didn't quite crest.

That would change.

He began to pump. In and out, each stroke taking him deeper, filling her, stretching her. The pulsing in her channel, the quivers and moisture of her impending climax, drenched him in sensations.

"You are mine." He chanted. His. His. His.

How could he ever have thought he could leave her behind? What foolishness ever led him to believe he could live without her by his side?

His barbarian human was made for him. The greatest treasure ever.

*And she's mine.*

To seal the revelation, he resorted to a practice of his ancestors. He bit her.

# Chapter Thirteen

*"Of course I believe in love at first sight. And while your grandpa at the time didn't, he sure changed his mind quick when my daddy caught us in the hayloft." – How Grandma got engaged.*

Something happened when Vile bit her, an epiphany, an alien infection, definitely an orgasm.

As Jilly's body crested and spasmed in the extreme delight only he seemed capable of delivering, it occurred to her that she loved this man, alien, whatever the hell he was.

So what if they'd known each other only a small time? She knew from experience, at least from her grandma, that love at first sight happened. In this case, all it took was a bite for her to finally admit it.

A bite to open her eyes to the fact Vile completed her. He brought her alive. He engaged all of her senses.

*I want him, not just as a lover, but as a friend, companion, everything.*

So what if he couldn't say the L word? Did he not show his own need for Jilly in other ways?

As he sucked at her punctured skin, his cock still thrusting into her trembling body, she heard him murmur, over and over, "Mine. All mine. My treasure."

How cute. Since the biting thing seemed to

be symbolic for him, she decided to see what would happen if she reciprocated. She chomped him back.

It got an interesting result.

One: he yelled and came, a molten gush of liquid within her that triggered a second smaller orgasm in her.

Two: once the tremors subsided, he murmured, his incredulity evident, "You bit me."

"Yup."

"Females aren't supposed to bite their males to mark them."

"This human one does. Got a problem with it?"

His blue eyes, glowing with a fierce light, met her gaze as he growled. "You are unlike anyone I've ever met." He grinned. "And I like that."

"Good, because you are stuck with me."

"Would it please your feminine sensibilities to know that you are my finest treasure?"

"It does please me." Immensely. But it also reminded her of something. "I'm sorry you had to trade the artifact to get me back."

An emotion crossed his face. Sheepishness mixed with pride. "And if I didn't?"

"What do you mean? I saw you give it to Snaggle Tooth."

"Not quite. While I did have the artifact on my person when making the exchange, the item I actually gave him was the bomb that destroyed his ship."

Jilly couldn't talk for a moment. "You mean you didn't give up a treasure for me after all?" So much for thinking she mattered more.

"No. But before you get angry. I should admit, but will deny if my family ever asks, that I would give everything I own to keep you. You are now the only acquisition that matters."

His compliment didn't entirely erase her irritation with him. "You owe me, purple dude."

"A warrior owe a female debt?"

"Damned straight. And when I call you on it, I expect you to deliver."

"I am an expert at delivering," he said with a suggestive leer.

He was.

Especially when it came to surprise because, when she accidentally slipped at one point and said during the throes of passion, "I love you," to her shock, he said the words she thought she'd never hear. "I love you, too, my sweet barbarian."

# Epilogue

*"Only the common steal. Acquisition is a fine art. And if you don't agree, then I shall show you how I like to paint with the blood of those who would think to insult me." – Vhyl's reply to those who dare question his career choice.*

Vhyl should have known Jilly would eventually collect on the debt she claimed he owed her. Yet, he would have never expected the level of cruelty she'd indulge when she did.

No wonder his mother adored her. His human was delightfully evil when she put her mind to it.

"No," he protested even though he knew he'd lose.

"Come on, Vile, please."

His woman could beg all she wanted. He wouldn't do it. "I will not wear that ridiculous hat."

"But it's Christmas."

"I agreed to deliver your bloody trees to your new friends," potted, not chopped off and killed, "However, a warrior does not stoop to wearing disguises that draw from his awesome nature, especially not in front of the enemy."

"Some of them are your cousins."

"And your point is?"

"I forget how messed up the family system is in your culture."

"Evolved you mean."

"Whatever. You will wear the outfit. You owe me." She planted her hands on her hips and glared.

"You can't be serious. I can't believe you would waste the ridiculous debt I owe you to have your way in this."

Yet waste it she did.

Despite the fact he'd probably have to engage in a murderous spree, Vhyl wore what she called the Santa Claws suit—which he couldn't figure out given it had no claws but did boast a ridiculous beard, spectacles, and a red hat with a fluffy ball on the end.

To please her, he agreed to the black boots, red breeches, and hat, but he drew the line at the padded jacket and the rest.

Carrying a sack on his back, Vhyl approached the home of his enemy—councilor Tren.

His unwilling host also wore a scowl. "Welcome to my frukxing home," he snarled.

"Manners," said the human female at his side with a jab at the former assassin's ribs.

Vhyl waited for him to murder her. No one berated Tren.

To his eternal surprise, the big male sighed. "You know I am going to need to wreak violence on something after this."

"So long as you do it outside," his wife, Megan, replied. "Now, try again."

In a dull monotone, Tren said, "Thank you

for coming to our Christmas celebration. Won't you come in?"

It took a poke in his back for Vhyl to step over the threshold. One usually didn't willingly enter the lair of a murderous beast.

Jilly didn't hesitate. She flounced in and was immediately hugged by Megan, who squealed, "I am so happy to finally meet you in person. Come with me so I can introduce you to everyone."

As Tren's wife led the way, chatting with Jilly, who looked way too tempting in a red velvet dress that showed too much leg—he had plans to blind anyone who looked too long at the exposed skin—Tren muttered under his breath for Vhyl alone. "Later. You, me and the other males will hit the training ring and pummel each other to counter the humiliation our mates subject us to."

Vhyl grinned. So he wasn't the only one who had to deal with a bossy human. Good to know. Perhaps he could score some pointers on how to handle Jilly.

Or not.

It soon became clear when he entered the gathering space filled to the brim with people that while the males, and a few of the matrons, were born and bred Aressotles through and through, the humans sprinkled among them had changed the nature of such a gathering.

For one, no one was fighting. At least not with weapons.

But the insults flowed easily. "Hey, Vhyl, what bet did you lose that forced you to wear that ridiculous hat?"

To that he had an easy response. "At least I can take off the hat later on. You're stuck with that face for life." An insult Makl frowned at.

A little boy, his skin a light mauve but his lungs as fierce as any warrior from his home world, waved a sword as he rode the shoulders of Brax.

Louisa, whom he'd previously met, watched her gallivanting mate with a forbearing expression while her hands rested on her distended belly. It seemed Brax and Xarn proved fruitful.

Later on at dinner, the conversation flowed, and Vhyl caught snippets of it, especially his mate's reaction to Megan's toast.

"I just want to say thank you all for coming—and not spilling any blood on the floors. It's a bitch to scrub out. I know it's not easy to get so many of you warriors in one place without a murder happening."

"Yet," Tren added in an ominous tone.

"Oh, stop it with the tough guy act, or you won't be getting any pie later."

What kind of dessert could have the renowned assassin clamp his lips tight?

Megan continued. "This Christmas, I'd like to give thanks for the fact our purple husbands—"

"Warriors."

"Mercenaries."

"Assassins."

"Acquisition specialists."

"—whatever, abducted us and showed us how good life could be despite our different cultures."

"Hold on a second. You mean to say you were all abducted?" Jilly's eyes rounded.

"Of course. Didn't Vhyl tell you?"

He shrugged when his mate peered at him. "I told you we take what we want."

"Well, except for Megan. She was an Accidental Abduction," Tren stated.

"Which I resent. If you ask me, I was the best thing that ever happened to you." Megan glared at her spouse, but not too angrily given she plopped into his lap and draped her arms around his neck.

"Best accident ever," Tren replied, his express soft, for his mate only. Everyone else got a glare that dared them to repeat his admission.

"Ha, my introduction to Jaro was anything but an accident. His was an Intentional Abduction," Aylia announced.

"Only because I allowed it," Jaro retorted as he juggled a pair of babies who slept soundly, one in the crook of each arm.

"Mine was a Dual Abduction, by dumb and dumber," Louisa announced.

"Hey, I resent that. I would have kept you all to myself if dumber here hadn't insisted we share."

"Insisted, ha? You could have never bested me, and you know it."

"Idiots," Makl replied with a shake of his head. "I am the only one with any pride to admit mine was a purely Mercenary Abduction. I saw Olivia and had to have her."

"Oh please, you only came after me because Aunt Muna told you to get a nanny for Mren."

"The reason why doesn't matter. The fact of the matter is, you're mine."

"No. You're mine."

As they bickered, Jilly looked at the last couple in the group. "What of Dyre? Didn't I hear you were the do-gooder black sheep of the family? I can't see you kidnapping a woman and making her love you."

Dyre straightened in his seat. "In my case, I attempted a Heroic Abduction. And succeeded. For the most part."

Betty shook her head. "While laying waste on the way. My dear mate means well, but he really isn't cut out to be a hero."

"And what of you, Jilly? How would you classify your abduction?"

All the eyes at the table turned Jilly and Vhyl's way, and he could see her stumped for an answer.

"Given I acquired her during the barbaric Earth custom known as Kris-mass, I'd say hers was a Holiday Abduction."

"More like chaotic, but at least it had a happily ever after," Jilly added, squeezing his thigh under the table.

"I like hers," little Mren announced. "It has presents."

Indeed it did. In Vhyl's case, it was the gift of love, an emotion he now understood and would kill to keep.

*Mine. Forever.*

## The End

# Special Holiday Treat

*\*\*\*Originally written as a blog post, this is a mini story featuring Megan and Aylia, and their first Christmas with their purple men. For those who've not met them, Megan is the human from the first book Accidental Abduction, and Aylia is the heroine in Intentional Abduction.*

Aylia watched the ending of the video, an odd piece full of singing, laughter, and garish decorations. She turned to face her friend, Megan, a puzzled expression creasing her face. "This human holiday, Kris-mass, you celebrate it every year?"

"Yup." Megan bobbed her head. "I'll bet you probably celebrated several with your human parents before you got abducted and given to the Zonians. It's the one Earth holiday I miss."

"Because of the gifts?"

Megan smiled widely. "Presents are good, but also because it was the one time of the year people were determined to be happy, or at least fake it."

"Why?"

"Why? Well, because it was Christmas. A time when families got together and ate too much rich food. An excuse for cousins to run wild through Grandma's house while aunts and uncles got drunk on spiked eggnog. Good old-fashioned family fun."

Despite the description, Aylia wasn't sure she quite got it, but her friend seemed enamored of the tradition. "If you love this holiday so much, then why not tell Tren? I am sure he would celebrate it for you."

Megan scrunched up her nose. "I could, I guess. I never thought of it. I mean, seriously, can you imagine Tren and Jaro decorating a tree or shopping for gifts?"

"No, but then again, I never imagined Jaro doing a lot of things," Aylia replied. "Did you know he picked a flower for me yesterday?"

"What's the big deal about that?"

"He climbed down the cliff by the seaside and plucked the bloom from a lukinol nest. He even had the teeth marks to prove it."

A chortle made her friend's very pregnant belly jiggle. "Okay, that is messed up. But cute. Definitely cute. Tren's more likely to punch Jaro out to steal the flower than get it himself."

"I resent that. I am more likely to grab the bloom from his fist and push him off the cliff so he can't tattle," Tren boasted as he strode into the room, all six-foot-something purple feet of him. If Aylia didn't have a purple warrior of her own as a mate, she might have found him more impressive.

"Aren't you just romantic?" Megan grumbled.

"Actually I am," Tren announced with a pleased grin that showed off his pointed teeth. "Jaro, stop dragging your feet and bring it in."

A curse followed the order, along with an

odd scraping and…was that the jingling of bells?

Aylia watched the doorway with interest and couldn't stop her mouth from dropping open as Jaro came in pulling something big and green behind him. Adorned in colorful balls and shiny tinsel, it looked an awful lot like a Kris-mass tree, just like the ones from the film Megan made her watch.

Tren helped his brother hoist and prop the holiday decoration against a wall, and then they both stood back to reveal the ugliest, bent-branched tree in existence.

"Wait, I forgot something." Tren yanked a box from his pocket before he dropped to his knees and rummaged around the lower branches. A moment later hundreds of little multi-colored lights ignited.

Aylia couldn't supress a giggle of delight. "It's so ugly it's beautiful," she exclaimed.

Megan burst into noisy tears.

Alarm crossed Tren's face as he crossed the room to sweep his mate into his arms. "What is wrong? Did I not get it right? I specifically told those idiots Brax and Xarn to get an authentic tree. Do I need to beat them again?"

"The tree is perfect," Megan sniffed.

"Then what is it? There are presents for it, too, I swear. Lots of them in that shiny paper just like the videos."

"Oh no," Megan moaned.

Tren looked at Aylia in bafflement, and she shrugged. She didn't know what ailed her pregnant friend, but she did know that she certainly didn't want to turn into such an emotional wreck as her pregnancy progressed. She'd hate to have to kill herself for being such an idiot.

Arms wrapped around her from behind as Jaro snuggled into her back, his hands coming to rest over her slightly rounded belly. "What do you think?" he whispered in her ear, his warm breath never failing to bring a delighted shiver.

"I think it is a fine gift," she replied as she turned in his arms. "Even if I don't quite understand the whole holiday idea. Although, I am not averse to the idea of presents. But I have nothing to give you."

"Oh, I can think of a few things," he said with a leer that made her laugh.

A yell distracted her from that pleasant train of thought, but this time it came from Tren, not Megan.

"What the frukx? Why are my feet wet?" Tren bellowed.

"Don't you yell at me," Megan shouted back. "It's all your fault. You made me so damned happy with the Christmas tree that I forget to mention when you walked in that the baby is coming."

"What!" The shouted exclamation from the three of them had Megan smiling smugly.

"Ha, you might have gotten me a tree and presents, but even you can't beat me giving you a son for Christmas," she said triumphantly. "Oh, and by the way, I think you'd better wash your hands quick because this baby is dying to get out."

And then the most amazing thing happened. The renowned assassin, a male who terrified whole galaxies, who could torture alien slavers while eating an eleven-course feast, dropped to the floor in a dead faint.

Megan howled with laughter, and Aylia joined her, a laughter that increased tenfold when Jaro's face creased in disgust when he had to step through the wet puddle to slap his brother awake.

In the end, the baby was born—the normal way through the vulva—which personally Aylia found more terrifying than the idea the child would chew its way through the abdomen like Megan feared. Things the size of Kewla fruits should not come out of holes that small. But she did have to admit she found the wrinkly creature with lavender skin, shockingly blue eyes, and a pair of lungs to deafen even the most stalwart kind of cute.

Although not as cute as Jaro holding the little bundle with awe on his face. She slid her arms around his waist as they stared into their nephew's face.

"What a fine son," he said before handing it back to the beaming parents.

The ferocious love in Tren's eyes for both his mate and child made Aylia warm inside. And that's when she blurted it out.

"We're having girls."

"Excuse me? What did you say?" Jaro's voice emerged faint.

"We're having girls, as in two of them. Isn't

that exciting?"

And, for the second time that day, a big purple warrior crashed to the ground while Aylia gaped on in disbelief. Then giggled.

"Merry Kris-mass to me," she chortled. "I am going to have so much fun with this now."

"Merry Christmas to us all," Megan added. "Now where's my presents?"

## The End

**Author's Note:** I hope you enjoyed this latest story in the Alien Abduction series. If you did, I'd love it if you took a moment and left a review. To know when my next story will be available, then please visit my website at http://www.evelanglais.com

Thank you for reading. ~ Eve